C000143407

ONE WAY
PASSAGE

ONE WAY
PASSAGE

Sharon L. Tocchini

Copyright © Sharon L. Tocchini

All rights reserved. No part of this book may be reproduced in any form or by any electronic or mechanical means, including information storage and retrieval systems, without permission in writing from the publisher, except by reviewers, who may quote brief passages in a review.

ISBN: 978-1-64606-739-8   (Paperback Edition)
ISBN: 978-1-64606-740-4   (Hardcover Edition)
ISBN: 978-1-64606-738-1   (E-book Edition)

Some characters and events in this book are fictitious. Any similarity to real persons, living or dead, is coincidental and not intended by the author.

Book Ordering Information

Phone Number: 347-901-4929 or 347-901-4920
Email: info@globalsummithouse.com
Global Summit House
www.globalsummithouse.com

Printed in the United States of America

In Memory of
my Father

Leo Paul Tocchini

The most loving and
positive influence my
life has ever had.

Lord,
give me the guidance
to know
when to hold on
and
when to let go
and the grace
to make the right decision
with dignity.

Reinhold Niebuhr

"Every adversity holds within it the seeds
of an undeveloped possibility."

Napoleon Hill

CHAPTER ONE

Kelly felt the fatigue of the hectic day nag at her body and mind. She knew Danny was tired too. She gently laid the small limp body of her son in his bed, covering him with the worn yellow baby blanket he loved.

She stroked his thick, wavy, chestnut brown hair as he grabbed and snuggled close to his beloved teddy bear who had been sitting in the corner of the crib. The bear's eyes were the same dark brown as Danny's, only the long, soft lashes that trimmed Danny's big eyes made all the difference. He looked like his daddy, she thought as she kissed his warm forehead and covered him with another lightweight blanket.

Kelly's mind raced and refused to slow down even though her body ached and wanted to rest as she lay on her blue satin bedspread. Her head ached as well. The memory of Danny's birth had repeated itself thousands of times over the past four years.

Kelly could still see Dr. Norman, the pediatrician, walk into the room with his head lowered a bit as he pulled the curtain around the bed and stood at her bedside in his white lab coat over light blue scrubs. In a low, almost cowardly, monotone voice he had said, "Danny's Apgar scores were not normal; that's a gauge of how well the baby looks and responds immediately after birth," he explained, "and Danny has most likely been born with brain damage."

Kelly turned toward Dr. Norman as she fought back the tears, and in a voice that was so meek she knew he could barely hear her ask, "what kind of brain damage?" She looked down at the satin-soft bundle in her arms. Daniel Robert Ashley, the most beautiful baby in the whole world she had thought, and now Dr. Norman was telling her he had a defect, a serious one. She felt fear grip her, as she watched this innocent, tiny being sleeping in her arms. Her mind raced with fear as she wondered what would the future hold for her precious infant and for their family?

Jason had repeated his wife's question, as it was evident from her tears she was too upset to continue the conversation. "What kind of brain damage?"

Dr. Norman had directed his attention to Jason who stood beside Kelly's bed, opposite the doctor. "We will not know that for some time yet. Tests must be done, X-rays, and MRI's taken. We will of course, wait until the baby is a bit older and stronger. We cannot tell to what degree your baby will be handicapped until then."

She recalled that Dr. Norman's voice thundered in her mind, as her memory conjured up the moments from four years ago. She could vividly see and feel herself reliving that moment as if in a dream. The memory was painful each and every time it reoccurred. Why wouldn't the memories go away? she questioned. They were not at all welcome within her head. She struggled mentally to evict them from her mind, but they continued nevertheless. Her tears now began to roll across her face and onto the pale blue satin pillow as her heart broke anew each time she relived this moment.

Kelly recalled Jason and she had looked at each other with questions in their eyes. Jason took her hand in his and squeezed it gently as if to reassure her it was nothing and it would all go away.

"How could this be?" she remembered saying in disbelief.

"Kelly, try to take it easy," the doctor said as he moved to the side of her hospital bed and put his large hand on her shoulder. "This doesn't mean the baby will be different from any other baby. He'll most probably only learn at a slower pace than other children..." He then turned to Jason. "Jason, if you wish to talk later, please call me at the office." He turned back to Kelly once more as she was visibly upset. "Kelly dear, please try to settle down."

The tears streamed silently down her face as she stared into the empty space in front of her. She became more upset each time she heard "handicapped" repeated inside her head. Her sweet tiny, helpless baby was handicapped. She watched as Dr. Norman glanced at Jason and then pushed through the flimsy curtains to leave the room.

Jason gently wiped the tears from her eyes with his monogrammed handkerchief and leaned over to kiss her forehead ever so gently as he spoke to her softly.

"Sweetheart, we don't know to what degree Danny will be handicapped. Dr. Norman said Danny will probably only learn at a slower pace, and I'm sure there are schools to help Danny learn. Let's try to think as positively as possible for now, okay?"

He sat on the bed next to her for quite some time. She knew he was doing his best to comfort her. She felt like he was coaching a small child into allowing the doctor to give a shot which everyone knew would hurt. He kept saying the situation wasn't as bad as she was making it out to be, but Kelly could see through Jason's eyes, clear to his heart. He was as hurt and upset by this terrible news as she was.

Kelly closed her eyes, hoping it was only a bad dream. She leaned her head with its reddish-blond hair onto the soft hospital pillows that lay behind her. She knew her nose had become red, and the few freckles on her fair skin were almost hidden.

She remembered it had been such a joyous event for which she and Jason had planned so carefully. *Planned Parenthood*, she remembered thinking with a sneer. Who could ever possibly plan for this? Their sweet, tiny boy, handicapped at birth with a serious brain defect.

She reminisced that they had both waited and planned so carefully, for so long. They had wanted everything to fall in the right place, at the right time. The college degrees and careers first, a home, time to spare, and money to afford the finer things, then the family.

Four years since that moment had passed and now she knew what the future held for her precious bundle, Jason and herself. It had been an endless stream of doctor appointments for tests, exams and therapy sessions, with no end in sight.

Danny was physically the size of a four year old, but he was only a year old mentally because of the retardation he suffered when he was born. However, Kelly carried her little boy around as if he were one, but her body yelled out to her that Danny was four and much too large and heavy. Carrying him around most of the day at the doctor's office had been hard on her back and legs, and they throbbed from the workout they had received.

She wondered how she would explain to Jason what Dr. Townsend had explained to her only two hours earlier. There was so much to tell, and she was never good with words. She never had much to say and preferred to keep her conversations brief. It seemed that doctors always knew what to say in such few sentences. Dr. Townsend was the most congenial of all the neurosurgeons they had chosen to work with, and he too, was brief and to the point. She continued to toss and turn as she wondered if the briefness of their explanations were part of their medical training or part of their errors and omissions training.

The reality of the outside world no longer had any meaning. The terrorist bombings, nature's devastation, global warming and the President's inauguration had no significance once her world collapsed in on her.

Her degree in business administration had done nothing to prepare her for such heartache. Maybe if it had been a degree in nursing or child care she had gone after originally. No, nothing could prepare her for what she had been though with Danny in the last four years, she thought.

She closed her eyes, and her mind flashed back in time once again. The vision of Danny's birth had been repeated within her mind so many times it came easily. No matter how she tried, it seemed impossible to dismiss it.

To carry this little human being inside her for nine long months, feeling it move and grow, even hiccup, had her anticipating a baby like anyone else's. Was that too much to ask or expect. When they learned about Danny's defect, she also learned that everyone in these same types of circumstances felt guilty, inadequate and imperfect when your offspring turned out to be abnormal at birth. Had she done something to put her small infant at risk before he was conceived, she wondered.

Kelly's mind forced the scenes of the past on her. She could once again feel the frenzied panic to get to the hospital on time in commute traffic. They had timed the pains so carefully and all of a sudden hard labor had begun.

She tossed and turned upon her bed as if trying with equal force to push out the memories. Her long, light red hair tossed around behind her as she struggled to rest.

Her thoughts shifted. It was Jason who had been her strength through all she had endured thus far. He must have learned to expect the unexpected in his law school training. Had he also been taught to hide what you really feel inside, all the while convincing the outside audience to believe what you wanted them to. Deep inside she knew Jason had taken the brain damage of his first born son extremely hard. He rationalized constantly why this was happening to the two of them. He gently reminded her much too often that everything happens for a reason. He might have believed that in his head and in his heart, but she was confused and upset that her son was not what she had expected and less than perfect. She knew in her heart that she had begun questioning God at this time in her life. It all seemed so unfair and unjust.

Tears began to well in the corner of her eyes as she lay on her back staring at the blank, white ceiling. She wiped the wetness that slid down the side of her face with the tips of her fingers and tossed to her side again.

She closed her eyes and could picture the tiny, wet, creature wrapped in a well-used hospital baby blanket, being handed to her shortly after birth. She remembered the elation she felt that washed away the tremendous pain she had experienced only moments before.

She had explored in her mind all the possibilities of what might have gone wrong, over and over again. Nothing had occurred out of the ordinary during the birth. They had decided not to use drugs of any sort and had practiced LaMaze and natural child-birth for the birth of their first born. Everything had gone well. The doctor and nurses seemed to share in the excitement, and Jason could hardly wait to hold his own flesh and blood.

"Are all newborn babies this beautiful," she had asked at the time, "or just mine?" It was a rhetorical question, of course, she remembered thinking.

The happiness, the feeling of a job well done, the completeness, the oneness she and Jason felt was shot to hell when Dr. Norman, had given them the news.

Again, she tossed and turned on the cool blue satin bedspread as the vivid memories haunted her. Although she felt mentally and emotionally exhausted, she could not fall asleep. She was a small woman of five foot four inches and one hundred and fifteen pounds, but, nevertheless, the mattress creaked as she constantly turned from one side to the other. If only I could sleep as soundly as babies do, she thought. She didn't hear a sound from Danny's room. He had fallen asleep.

She recalled Danny had been especially good about all the different tests, time and time again. She knew if it had been her that had been poked, prodded, wired to, dye dumped into, X-rayed, watched, and monitored by every machine possible, she would have gone crazy by now. It had been nothing but a bad dream for the last four years. Their sweet, little Danny. He was such a happy baby, and all that he had been through couldn't change that. She could remember, as her mind flashed to the past once again, the cold, antiseptic room in which he had been placed when later tests had been done. The sight of her tiny son being covered with small rubber objects with connecting wires to record his mental and physical reactions. Danny acted as if it was just another game, and he seemed to love the attention he received from the doctors and nurses and the music they played just for him.

Danny appeared to have become quite attached to his neurosurgeons, Dr. Hess and Dr. Townsend. It seemed as though he saw them as often as he did his own daddy. Danny would get excited and smile when either of them entered the room.

She recalled the many, many tests he had been through and the endless stream of doctors. She wondered if any of it would ever end, and then focused on what Jason would think of the news Dr. Townsend had shared with her earlier today? She couldn't wait to tell him. She pulled the bedspread from Jason's side of the bed, up and over to cover herself. The satin felt cool to her skin, and yet the warmth from the weight of the covering allowed her to feel secure and she gradually slipped into sleep.

To everything there is a season,
and a time to every purpose
under the heaven.

Ecclesiastes 3:1

CHAPTER TWO

Kelly woke to the sound of Danny plunking on his toy piano. She wondered, as she lay listening, if he knew he could not get past the expanding gate which stood guard at his door for protection and, therefore, preoccupied himself with his toys. She never quite knew what and how much Danny was comprehending of the world around him. She did know that he was an exceptionally good baby and cried only when he was hurt. She felt fortunate in that respect. Many people had expressed to Kelly their surprise at how happy a "handicapped" child could be. Kelly had learned how ignorant of handicapped children the general public actually was. They seemed to always connect the word handicapped with freak, and it was still very difficult for Kelly and Jason to get a baby-sitter if her mother was not available. Kelly knew many people felt that distance was the best policy when it came to a handicapped child, and she did her best to cope with what she knew was simple ignorance.

She was grateful Danny's condition was not as readily noticeable as some of the other handicapped children she had seen at the testing centers. She was also grateful she did not have to deal with the revolting looks and offensively murmured remarks of the uneducated, inexperienced human beings who felt anything out of the ordinary should be shut away in an institution or a cage. It was amazing to find the human race could be so inhumane, cruel, and stupid. Maybe she wasn't being fair, she thought, I guess it depends which side of the fence you're on. She felt a twinge of unfairness come over her. She was aware a great deal more was being done to educate the general public about mental retardation, and reduce the unnecessarily mean reactions such children had to endure. Maybe with time people will be more accepting and generous in their nature concerning children who were different from the norm, what ever that might be, she admonished herself.

Kelly would have loved to have more children if she knew they could all be as happy as Danny, but she would not consider pregnancy again until she knew what had caused Danny's brain damage, and she would not be submitting another child to the same fate.

She knew this was much to Jason's dismay, since he said repeatedly that he wanted more children now. He said he felt safe about having more children, but then he had always be the more optimistic of the two, she thought. Kelly knew she and Jason had gone through a period of feeling guilty and then of accusing each other. But reason won out, and they then went on searching for a cause, hopefully to replace the guilt they both felt for Danny's condition. She was pleased she had chosen Jason as her partner. He was so much stronger than she and more rational. She knew her emotions got the best of her most of the time. She was aware Jason didn't blame her for her female characteristics, and did his best to be understanding. After all, the fact that he had four sisters, and he had been the only boy, must have helped, and she was grateful for that.

She had retraced every moment of pregnancy and labor in her mind over and over again. Family trees had been reviewed for any aberrant characteristic or gene which might have lead to Danny's defect. Nothing had given the answer to Danny's fate. Then finally, the guilt was dismissed. Their life had now taken on only one purpose— to make Danny as whole a person as possible, if not complete. If he was hurt or damaged, so were they, and for them to be healthy and complete, Danny must also be.

Kelly opened her eyes slowly and felt the urge to close them again and sleep on in the escape from reality if only for a few more hours. She glanced over at the clock next to her bed. Jason would be home in an hour, or so she hoped. He worked long hours, sometimes too long. Occasionally, she felt overwhelmed when he failed to come home until late and she had to deal with everything by herself. She reluctantly tossed the cover off and slowly got up to remove Danny's gate from the doorway and rescue him from his limited world within his room.

"Hello, sweetheart. Did you have a nice nap?"

Danny smiled. "Lok." He pointed to his piano. He spoke very little because the words didn't form well on his tongue, if at all, and he wasn't often understood. Kelly could see that Danny would often get frustrated by not being understood, so she guessed Danny chose not to speak.

"That's a nice piano, and you play so beautifully," she said with a tone of love and understanding in her voice. "Do you want to help Mommy fix dinner?" Danny held up his hands and waited for his mommy to pick him up. It was evident he had found ways to communicate without words, just like other children do with words. They headed down the stairs and towards the kitchen.

The brain damage had affected all of Danny's physical aspects, but it was Dr. Hess who had told Kelly and Jason many times, that he felt he was mentally getting through to Danny, even when Danny appeared unresponsive. He also told Kelly and Jason he could sense this feeling from what he saw in Danny's eyes. Danny had no problem directing his eyes as did most other brain damaged children. They were large, deep brown, almost black, and seemed to be trying to say something whenever the tests were being administered. Kelly watched closely for this communication each time the two of them were together.

None of the other doctors agreed. Only Jason and Kelly had felt the warmth and communication from Danny's eyes. Dr. Hess had tried every new test and worked more with Danny than any of the other children at the hospital. He had put hope into Jason's and Kelly's hearts from the moment they had met him.

Kelly felt he was the most optimistic doctor they had talked to regarding Danny's condition.

The other doctors had said the brain damage was permanent and nothing could be done. Only Dr. Hess tried everything under the sun. He had put Danny through every known test. Kelly often wondered if it was his youth which gave him so much hope, or did he actually think something could be done.

Kelly put Danny on the floor in the kitchen with his own set of plastic pots and pans. He would play and bang the pans together. Kelly knew he didn't realize they were the type of objects his Mommy was using to cook dinner, though this was his way of helping.

The aroma of pork chops filled the room with their delicious smell, and the beans bubbled softly while the potatoes fried in the hot oil on the next burner. Kelly and Danny were sitting at the table when Jason opened the door. He walked over and picked up Danny and kissed him hello.

"Hi honey. Hello, Danny. How's Daddy's big fellow? I see you and Mommy are fixing Daddy's favorite."

Kelly knew Jason loved to mix the beans, potatoes, and applesauce together. It was his all-time favorite meal.

"What's the occasion, Mommy?"

"Danny and I have some news for you tonight. Go wash up, and we'll tell you at dinner."

"Okay, it's a deal." He put Danny in his high chair and went to wash his hands. "I'll be right back, little man." Jason kissed the top of Danny's head before turning to go.

Kelly put dinner on the table. The blessing was said as they all held hands.

"Okay, tell me the news," he said as he reached for the platter of juicy, golden-brown pork chops.

"Well, today when Danny went to see Dr. Hess, he had special X-rays taken. A ventriculogram, I think he said. The X-ray outlines the chambers of the brain on the film and shows the normal appearances of the brain's cavities. Dr. Hess said Danny's X-rays were not normal, and there is a possibility of a brain tumor."

Jason stopped eating and looked at Danny for a moment and then at Kelly. "What does all this mean?"

"The doctor said maybe, just maybe, this might be Danny's problem. More tests will have to be done. Next week he is going to give Danny an arteriogram and extensive electro... encphalo... graph. Don't ask me exactly what those are. It's hard enough to remember how to say their names. Dr. Hess doesn't want us to get our hopes too high only to be disappointed. He said, if it is a brain tumor inside Danny's brain, it may be possible to remove it completely, and make Danny almost, if not completely, normal. He thinks it's affecting the motor parts of his brain, but he's not sure about the mental disability." She spoke quickly as if it were rehearsed and she worried about missing a line if she didn't hurry through it.

Jason's mouth turned to a large smile and his eyes glittered as if he were watching his favorite baseball team falling behind on the scoreboard and the coach had just put in the key player who could win the game for them.

"Jason," she said, feeling sudden terror, "what if the tumor is malignant?"

"We'll have to pray extra hard, I guess," he said while still watching Danny.

She could see the hope in Jason's eyes. "Jason, you're not listening. Dr. Hess cautioned us not to get our hopes up too high. He said that the tumor could be in such a place, and depth that they might not be able to reach it, and there is a possibility the operation might even make Danny physically disabled permanently. Paralyzed! Jason, do you hear me?"

Jason continued to stare at his little fellow.

"Jason, do you hear me?" She began to get angry with Jason and herself, "it's a very touchy thing. If only I could explain it the way he did to me." She looked down at the food in her plate that was growing cold while she was fighting back the tears. She had promised Jason sometime ago she would try to be stronger. It wasn't working.

"It's okay, sweetheart. I understand." He picked up the sweet, chubby, little hand smeared with applesauce between the fingers and kissed it. "I'll bet on the long shot every time" he said as he winked at Danny.

"Guess who's getting married next month?" Jason said as he turned his attention back to Kelly and the pork chops.

"Kathy," she replied as she looked up from her plate.

"Nope, Wendy."

"Wendy? Next month? She didn't even have a boyfriend last time I heard," Kelly said.

Jason finished chewing the last bite of his meat before replying. "She just met the fellow about a week ago and says she's madly in love. She calls him her soul mate. Love at first sight. I guess at nineteen you still believe in love at first sight." He laughed and returned to his dinner.

Kelly could tell he hadn't had lunch today by the manner in which he ate his dinner. He must be famished, she thought. "What's a soul mate?"

"She claims she knew this fellow in a previous life and that's how she's so sure, so soon." He paused as if processing the thought. "When she talks of him, her face has a certain radiance about it I've never seen her show before."

"Well, maybe she'll realize it's not love but lust before they actually get married," Kelly said cynically.

"Or," he stopped and looked directly into Kelly's eyes, "it is love at first sight, and we're just growing too old to believe in such fantasies. After all, I thought it was love at first sight when I met you, and it has continued to grow and blossom." He paused. "I do love you, you know."

She got up from the table and walked over to Jason, leaned over and kissed him. "I love you too, sweetheart. Now, would you like some dessert?"

"Sure," he said with a twinkle in his eye. "Right here, right now, and in front of Danny?" he said teasingly.

Kelly knew it was lovin' and not Jello he had on his mind. She pushed his arm away from around her waist.

"Dessert is chocolate cake and whipped cream, Jason Douglas. Do you or don't you want some?" She smiled, and although she blushed, she loved the flattery.

Kelly was the bashful, quiet type. She kept her knowledge and thoughts within. She was like a soft, timid kitten.

Jason and she got along like spring and summer. She came on quietly with much beauty. Jason came on strong, aggressive and lively. His outgoing ways overshadowed Kelly. She loved it, though. He was the social, lively one who brought active living to life. She was sometimes in awe of his lust for life.

Once Danny had been put to bed and the kitchen cleaned, Kelly sat down to relax. Jason was riffling through the newspaper, searching for the sports page and the scores of the high school basketball game.

"Jason, do you think Mom's silly notion about reincarnation has any credibility?"

"Well, in the first place," Jason said as he laid the paper in his lap, "it's evident you don't want to accept the concept."

"Come on, Jason, be fair. What on earth could someone have done in a previous life to cause such suffering in this life? Mom said that's what karma is." Kelly's voice began to quiver and her emotions began to take control.

"What's so silly about reincarnation? Is it easier to believe that we have evolved from an ape like creature or that Adam and Eve were thrown out of the Garden of Eden to go forth and populate the entire earth?" He stopped and watched for her reaction. She waited for him to continue as she knew he would. "Sweetheart, I don't know exactly what to believe, but Dr. Hess feels he is somehow reaching Danny mentally. Even we have felt Danny's communication through his eyes. I feel he knows and feels more than he can express verbally to us."

"I can't believe a just God would make any person suffer this way," Kelly said. "There's just got to be a reason for Danny's brain damage."

"What makes you so sure he's suffering? He's in no apparent pain." He lowered his voice. "Kelly, you really must stop looking for someone or something to blame. Danny isn't an unhappy child, is he?"

Jason the attorney was showing, she thought. When he started talking, he didn't stop until he felt he had gotten his point across.

"I think it's up to us to believe that what's happening to Danny and to us is happening for a specific reason. I wish you would try to believe things happen because they were meant to. There are no coincidences in life, honey." He patted her hand.

She could tell he realized he had raised his voice. He lifted her hand to his lips and kissed it gently.

"Come on. Let's watch the nine o'clock news and let the subject rest for now."

"Okay." She could feel the weight of the burden upon her shoulders once again. Each time she felt that ominous weight, her emotions seemed to run away and leave her rational mind behind.

Jason always had a way of ending a discussion, anyway. It was like he had just dismissed her from the room. He sometimes made her feel as if she spent her time foolishly worrying over things that amounted to nothing at all and if left alone they would just go away. Yet, his strength and self-assurance gave her strength. Still, she pondered the why of it all.

Chapter Three

1919

James sat at his wooden desk concentrating intensely on the words he put on his finest stationary to his dearest friend, his mother.

He was well aware his friends at college felt his affections for his mother were in excess of the normal maternal relationship, but he didn't much care. He had never considered himself average or normal, but unique and distinctive. It was that same, very special person, his mother, who had instilled confidence and self-assurance.

His father had died at a very early age, and his mother was the only person he remembered as having always been there for him. She had shaped his atmosphere into a loving, positive world. Although she had been an authoritarian, she still remained his best friend and always would.

He wrote with care, choosing the news he sent home with the utmost attention. She had not yet grown accustomed to her boy being a young man out in the world on his own.

3 November 1919

Dearest Mother

All is well here, although it is cold and the snow is deep. I do hope all is well with you. I miss you and your companionship and hope Aunt Martha is good company for you. I'm so pleased she decided to come stay with you, since I'll be away for what seems like an eternity.

I miss you terribly and will look forward to coming home for Christmas.

I do enjoy it here and feel privileged to have the opportunity to study, but that doesn't mean I miss you any less.

The fellows here at the college are congenial, and I have made some good friends already. It's a different environment, but better, nevertheless, than living on the outside in the weary, unstable world. I feel somewhat sheltered from what actually takes place according to the newspapers.

Most of the students are very concerned about the health of President Wilson but have positive attitudes of a better and brighter world to come once this graduating class is released to conquer the masses and make their dreams a reality. It's probably a good thing we have several years to go before that happens. However, I'm not sure the world will be ready for some of us even then.

I do wish you could meet some of the fellows here. I'm sure you would define them as rascals but would love them just the same. Well, Mother dearest, I must end this letter shortly, since I promised to go with the fellows today. Charles Faraday has been given the family Model T, and I have been given the blessing of the first ride, after I have cranked the thing up, of course. I'm leery of cranking ever since old Buzz broke his arm doing it last year, but don't worry, your loving son shall be careful.

Take care, dear Mother.

Your loving son,
James

"Come on, James. Charles will get impatient and leave," yelled his roommate.

"Charles won't go anywhere without us, Henry. Don't get so upset. After all, bashful Charles couldn't meet a female without the two of us to sweep the young ladies off their feet, now could he?" said James as he rose from the desk.

"Charles may not be the best-looking fellow on campus and his being extremely bashful doesn't help, but now that he has a car, things might be different for him."

"Right, ol' man. We'll just make sure they are, won't we? After all, what are friends for?" He winked at Henry before he reached to open the door.

"Does your mother know how vain you are, James Connectivich?" asked Henry who was not as self-assured as James.

"Yes. As a matter-of-fact, I just finished writing her to remind her how lucky she is to have such a son. Come on. Charles is waiting."

The sun's rays were warm, causing tiny rivulets to flow from beneath the two-foot blanket of snow still remaining from the last fall two weeks before.

Henry laughed at James as they headed toward the Model T. "It's a good thing you're an only child, James, or you might encounter competition from your siblings."

"You could be right," he said as he patted Henry's back. Now, crank the Ford, my good fellow." He then stepped high into the car. He smiled, pleased with himself that he had gotten out of the undesired chore.

"What took you two so long?" asked Charles. It was evident that he was irritated with them. "My mother prefers that meals be served on time, and that is difficult to do if the guests have not yet arrived," he said sarcastically. He released the emergency hand brake with more force than necessary. He shoved his foot against the low-speed pedal, and with a jolt, the car jerked loudly into the street.

"Yes, Charles, we are indeed sorry," said James, teasing again. He knew they would arrive long before dinner was to be served.

It wasn't riding weather with all this snow, but who could wait to try out the newly acquired toy thought James. The long ride in the open-air car would chill their bones, even though each of them wore heavy wool overcoats; but the tepid brandy Charles had promised at the home of his parents would soon warm them once again.

CHAPTER FOUR

5 February 1920

Dearest Mother,

I am disheartened more each day. It's so difficult to believe the hatred that flows among the American people. Gramma and Grampa would have been saddened to see that the America they sought out for freedom had turned out to be a prejudicial sideshow.

I think back at the lessons you taught me from the Bible when I was so very small. Did no one else learn them? Love thy neighbor as thy self, or does no one care to remember?

I know you are as troubled as I, and there is so little we can do about it, but the pain increases as do the injustices.

They have begun targeting our professors here at the college and watching their every move. They are also censoring every piece of written material that crosses the campus. This all seems so ludicrous. Before the professors will speak of their personal convictions, they close all the doors and windows to make sure no one other than the individuals in the room are within earshot. I wonder where it will all end. At least I hope it will all end someday.

Some of my best friends are Roman Catholic or Jewish, and they aren't any different from myself or anyone else. It is beyond my imagination what has gotten into the American people. It's not communism they're afraid of; it's their own shadow. I sit here and wonder how bad it will get before the American people will realize how ridiculous this has become. After all, didn't all the immigrants come to America, like Gramma and Grampa, knowing that all people from every land and religion were coming here with the same hopes and dreams? Isn't that what

Americanism is all about? It appears these dreams are developing into nightmares.

I'm so sorry, Mother dear, this letter is not one of cheer. My heart aches as I watch the people around me being criticized for a belief they hold sacred or a bloodline over which they have no control.

I think of you and Aunt Martha constantly, hoping this prejudice is far from your doorstep. At times, I wish I could be there to protect my two favorite ladies from the mean, cruel world.

Even a man such as Henry Ford has spoken out against the Jewish people. No one is free from censure. Dearest Mother, take care to not be swayed. Even ladies groups have been persuaded to change their opinions in these vicious times.

I will pray that God watches over you both. I send my deepest love and miss you terribly.

Your loving son,

James

October 1920

Henry stepped into the room, and said, "James, are you coming with us this afternoon?"

"What's on the agenda?" James said as he looked up from his books, and set down his pencil.

"One of Charles's chemistry classmates, Pete Longley, you know him; well, he's brewed up some bathtub gin in his cellar. He claims it's outstanding stuff."

"What's wrong, Henry? Tired of waiting for the bootleggers from Canada?" He shut his book with the pencil still in it. "All right, but just for a while."

"Sure. That's fine. Let's go."

James grabbed his raccoon coat from the wardrobe, and shut the heavy wooden door behind them, then hurried down the steps behind Henry. They rode their bicycles over to Charles's dorm and would then venture farther in the Model T.

The motor car bounced down the dirt road to a dark brown clapboard house with a red brick porch. As they arrived, the repugnant odor of burning leaves filled their nostrils as a neighbor disposed of the early autumn color.

"By the way, how's Mother dear, and what does she think of this Women's Suffrage, James?" Charles asked.

James's friends often teased him about the close, loving relationship he and his mother had, but it was always with affection. James sometimes wondered if there was also a bit of envy in the teasing, since such a close and tender kinship was indeed a rare thing. He accepted their remarks in good humor since he knew he was the worst tease of all.

"She's quite happy about it. I doubt there's a woman alive who doesn't want to be treated equally," he said, then winked at Henry. "That's old news, Charles, but on the other hand, I guess this presents a problem for you, doesn't it?'

"What problem?"

"Well, as these women acquire more and more independence, you won't be able to force that sweet girlfriend of yours into submission."

"I've never forced her or any other female into anything," he said feigning anger. Then he grinned, "Not that I haven't wanted to." Once they had arrived, Charles opened the screen door and forced his knuckles against the hard surface several times. The door opened, and a young colored girl answered.

"Is Pete at home?"

"Yes, sir. He's down in the cellar," she said as she opened the door wide and backed away.

Charles led the way to the pantry, opened the door, and headed past the shelves of culinary staples and down the stairs, followed by James and Henry. Their eyes took a moment to adjust to the darkness of the cellar. The many aromas present were agreeable. The strongest was that of alcohol and juniper berries. It was a moist warmth that hung in the air, and James detected the soft sound of bubbling nearby.

Pete turned and glanced at the footsteps descending the wooden steps. "Well, that must be Charles," he said.

"It must be the jeans that gave it away, right Pete?" replied Henry.

Charles was known by his friends to be the rebellious one of his group, since he appeared to love to be the opposite of what his well-to-do family stood for and would prove his point by any means possible. Recently, he had taken to wearing ragged, lightweight jeans, which he changed once a week, if then. His friends were well aware that several times it had been drawn to his and his family's attention by the school officials. It was seen as an open attack on

20

his father and his formal way of life. James remembered he had heard Charles say many times, he loved ruffling his father's feathers.

"Hi, Charles," Pete said as he turned back to his work.

"How's the gin coming?" Charles said as he reached the bottom of the steps.

"It's the best batch I've made yet. Come try it." He turned and noticed Charles had brought friends.

"You know my friends, James and Henry, don't you?"

"Yes, we've met before. Here, have a belt," he said, thrusting the ladle toward them, spilling some of the clear liquid over the edge. "This recipe is fantastic. You don't even need a chaser with it." His excitement spilling over as well.

James reached for the ladle. "Sure, I'll try some." He lifted the cupped spoon to his nose, and then he swallowed the contents. It flowed smoothly down his throat and spread a fiery warmth throughout his body once it hit bottom. He smacked his lips, rolled his eyes, and dropped to the floor, grasping at his throat with one hand and covering his eyes with the other. "I'm blind, I'm blind," he yelled.

"Damn," Pete said, astonished. He fell to the floor on his knees beside James. "Shit, I've heard of this sort of thing happening with bootlegged gin, but . . . Shit." He grabbed James's wrists and looked up at Charles and Henry in a panic. "What should we do?"

"What do you mean we? It's your brew?" said Henry.

James began to giggle and was soon on his back, laughing hysterically at his most recent victim.

Pete stood up and backed away. "Shit, I wish I had killed ya." His eyes glared with anger.

Henry and Charles were now laughing along with James.

"Come on, Pete," Henry said. "He was only joking."

Pete's eyes returned to normal, "He really had me scared." Pete watched James get up from the floor, and his face softened. "Maybe I'm not the bootlegger type," Pete said as he turned to his brew and scooped up a full cup with another ladle that sat nearby and thrust the brew down his throat. "Or maybe I shouldn't watch my victims die," he said with a cynical laugh. "Okay the joke's on me, but I owe you one, James."

"How about another drink of the magic potion?" James asked.

"Hell, you'll pay for the next cupful." Pete said with a grin, but meaning every word of it.

Charles looked at Henry and shrugged. It was evident to James that Charles had misjudged his classmate. He was not the same type of personality as these three and would not easily fit in with their free sense of humor.

Pete offered both Charles and Henry a generous drink.

"No, thanks," said Henry, as Charles accepted his. "We have to be getting back. I've got a lot of studying to do."

"Thanks. It's great stuff," said Charles as he wiped his mouth with the back of his hand and gave the ladle back to Pete. "Your brew could give Dutch Schultz some competition." He turned to his friends, "we really should be going."

"It was nice seeing you again, Pete," said James who knew his joke hadn't been totally appreciated.

The three turned to go. They began giggling as soon as they reached the porch and Pete was out of earshot.

"Are you going to the dance tonight, James?" asked Charles as he climbed clumsily into the car.

"Can we use the car for an all-night ride if we meet the right females, Charles?"

"Only if I get lucky, too."

"Henry, do you think we can pay someone to dance and hang all over Charles tonight?" James said with a grin.

"We'll find someone, even if it costs my life savings." Henry said and lightly slapped Charles on the back.

James turned the crank in front of the car and hurried to jump in as the motor turned over.

"Why in the hell didn't your father get a self-starter?" he asked Charles as his posterior hit the leather seat.

"Would you rather walk?" Charles responded, as he gave James a sideward glance, pushed the choke in, and proceeded down the road.

Great people are ordinary people
with extraordinary amounts of determination.

Author Unknown

CHAPTER FIVE

Several weeks passed, and many extensive tests had been administered to Danny. The doctors had had all the time they needed to make a final diagnosis on the new information brought to light from the ventriculogram and other tests.

It was a bright, sunny Wednesday morning, which helped the mood to be cheerful for this long-awaited day. Jason had taken the day off, and Gramma would soon arrive to baby-sit little Danny while Jason and Kelly went to the hospital to discuss with the doctors what, if anything, could and would be done.

The drive to the hospital seemed longer than usual. Kelly held Jason's hand, hoping the strength she derived from him would be there as it always seemed to be. They walked down the corridor with its pale green walls and dark tweed carpet, which they had traveled a hundred times before to confer with the doctors.

Jason opened the door, allowing Kelly to enter first, as always. The room was somehow different. Kelly searched the room; it had the same warm brown paneled walls, the same soft velour beige couches, the same thick, tweed, tightly knit carpet, and the same two doctors sitting about in the large brown velvet chairs opposite the small sofa. Then she noticed the large bouquet of beautifully colored flowers of every kind, or so it seemed, in front of the northern window standing on the long, tall table. They filled the air with a sweet, soft fragrance. Her heart seemed to stop for a second, as if in warning. She sensed that the flowers were put there to add cheer to a room, which had in the past, brought only bad news. She shut the thought from her mind and turned to greet the all too familiar doctors.

Dr. Hess was always brief and to the point. He was also an extremely attractive man. His skin was an olive color, and his hair was

24

dark brown. His deep, dark brown eyes seemed to look affectionately at the world outside, and all but his name made him look of Italian descent. He had a certain charisma about him that made Kelly feel very comfortable in his presence.

Dr. Townsend, on the other hand, gave the air of being totally professional, almost cold. He seldom smiled, and it appeared he took life and the quality of it extremely seriously, she thought. His small size and plain features made him look mad at the world. He hurried from place to place as if something could not wait a moment longer. He made Kelly nervous.

"Good morning, Dr. Hess, Dr. Townsend," Kelly said.

"Yes, it is a good morning," replied Dr. Hess, smiling.

After the greetings were exchanged, the meeting was ready to begin. Kelly sat close to Jason on the velour sofa. The warmth of his body was reassuring. She grabbed for his hand and squeezed tightly.

Dr. Hess stood as he began to speak. "It's been four long years for you both, and for the first time we have some news that does set Danny apart from the rest of his handicapped group. We have considered all the pros and cons of the results of the latest tests and have come to a conclusion, but hear us out totally before deciding Danny's fate." He paused. "We have found that Danny has a definite tumor at the base of his brain, and as far as we can tell, the tumor is deeply imbedded and growing at a moderate pace." He paused, picked up the package of X-rays, and while taking them from the envelope, walked over to the wall which appeared to have a three-dimensional mirror image to it within a narrow frame. Dr. Hess pushed the X-ray up into the frame, and the floral frosted design in the center disappeared. The mirror became an X-ray viewer, one of the newer features of hospital equipment. He pointed to the area at the base of the head to an object the size of a large walnut, easily visible in the X-ray.

"This is the tumor, which had not made itself visible until recently. We feel the tumor has begun to grow rapidly only within the last few months, and that is why we have not been able to see it until now. It has been a small knot like tumor lodged within the brain itself. We cannot tell how far inside the brain it is, how fast it's growing, or in what direction."

Dr. Townsend interrupted. "The theory is that it is affecting the motor parts of Danny's brain."

Dr. Hess sat on the edge of the cabinet directly under the viewer. "If we choose to operate, it will be difficult to predict the outcome. If the tumor is benign and is growing only outwardly, there is a good chance Danny could, with time, be as normal as any four year old. As you know, I have always felt I have been reaching Danny's mental capacities in our studies of his behavior. Dr. Townsend also believes this to be a possibility, now."

Dr. Townsend nodded his agreement.

"But if the tumor cannot be fully removed or if the operation is not successful, Danny could also become paralyzed in any part of his body, depending on the area of the brain in which the tumor has taken root."

Dr. Townsend took over the conversation as if his cue had been given. "The decision is totally yours to make. If the operation were to fail, Danny would probably have to be institutionalized for life. You could, of course, decide against the operation altogether, and Danny would continue with his classes for the handicapped. He would have to continue these classes for some twenty years, progressing at a very slow pace. We are not suggesting you decide one way or the other. This must be your decision. It must be noted that the odds are not stacked in Danny's favor and the operation is quite risky." Dr. Townsend glanced at Dr. Hess, giving him the floor again.

Dr. Hess left his place on the cabinet and began to walk around the room. "We understand that this will take a great deal of consideration before a decision is reached. We ask that you weigh all the risks we have mentioned. If you decide that we should operate, I suggest that it be soon before the tumor is allowed to grow much larger."

Kelly felt scared. She didn't like life-or-death decisions of any kind. "Will the tumor continue to grow if the operation is not performed?"

"If we treat it chemically, we may be able to retard its growth. It has only recently shown itself to be a rapidly growing tumor, but no one can tell for certain."

Dr. Hess's voice was not as positive as it usually was, she thought. Dr. Hess had often spoke to both of them of his profession as if it were a power that had been granted to him. Kelly now sensed uncertainty. He had said in the past he could not conquer death but could play a part in prolonging life or at least making what was left of it more worth living. He had once shared with Jason and Kelly that he felt about his work much like he felt about the masterpieces painted long ago. Never could they be recreated in their originality or beauty. Each was one of a kind to be marveled at for eternity. She also knew he, as a boy, had always been intrigued by the legend of Merlin who could do what no one else could. She could see him striving for the same, and that in itself was a power.

She didn't know if this scared her or instilled confidence that this was indeed the doctor who should be doing brain surgery on her little boy. After all, she wouldn't want someone who was unsure of himself and his abilities doing any type of surgery, let alone anything as delicate, dangerous, and definite as brain surgery.

Jason looked at both doctors, one and then the other. "That's it? That's all you can tell us?"

"Yes," said Dr. Hess. "I wish I could tell you more, but until we get into Danny's head, it's mostly speculation. I'm sorry, Jason."

Jason rose from the couch, gently pulling Kelly along. He reached out his strong hand towards Dr. Hess who took Jason's hand and shook it and then put his arm around Jason's shoulder. "It's a tough decision. Good luck," he said as he walked to the door with them.

As Jason and Kelly walked down the corridor the discussion seemed to have put the weight of the world on them.

The remainder of the day would be spent with the burden of deciding the fate of the life that had been entrusted to them.

They returned home to get Danny and take him to the park where he loved the sounds of the miniature train that chugged and heaved to carry young children around the park.

Kelly's mother would have a lunch packed and ready for the threesome.

CHAPTER SIX

1923

Back in his room, James finished his studies and prepared himself for the evening's festivities. The smell of sulfur filled the vicinity as he lit a cigarette. The smoke stung his throat as he inhaled.

His green eyes peered at the reflection of a blossoming young man. The thin blond hair and slender body were reminiscent of the boy his mother had reluctantly given up to the outside world to further his education, but the face had become one of a man which showed expressions of a new mind. His attitudes had expanded and changed as had his world outside of the small town of his boyhood.

He watched the gleaming image in the mirror before him primp for his evening out. He pulled tight on the black satin bowtie at his neck. He smiled at the handsome young man in the mirror. He was no longer naïve and enjoyed this newfound feeling of freedom of engaging with people his age and the wild life that college now offered. He knew that one day he would return to his small home town and the close security of concern, but, for now, he would learn and live as never before.

As thoughts of home and of his mother edged into his thought, he turned to his desk, snuffed out the cigarette, and sat down to write.

18 May 1923

Dearest Mother,

I think of you often and miss you a great deal. Father was a lucky gentleman to have won such a beautiful woman.

I have the opportunity to meet many young women here, but none of them compare to you, Mother dearest.

I know you would be shocked at the current fashions away from your secure small town, but as I watch for a woman such as yourself behind the short skirts, rolled stockings, and sleeveless gowns, I realize you are a rare one indeed.

I do hope one day to meet someone such as yourself to take as my wife, with your approval, of course.

Don't worry Mother, my mind and course of direction are not about finding a woman at this point in time. I am serious about my desire to become a medical doctor and am working diligently towards my goal. I look forward to returning home to open a medical practice, and most of all, to again be near to you. I do so miss you and the feminine influence you have always had on me.

This evening the fellows and I are going out on the town, but have no fear, dear Mother, I will keep in mind all the morals and principles you have taught me.

Please take care of yourself and Aunt Martha while I'm away, so that I may return to my two most favorite females in all the world.

Your loving son,
James

He hesitated before putting the letter into the envelope. He wasn't sure how his mother would respond to his being so openly interested in young women.

However, she would need to accept the idea one day anyway, since he had no intention of remaining a bachelor forever. He addressed the envelope quickly, as he realized the hour was getting late and the fellows would soon be calling for him.

Charles pulled the car to the curb and turned off the noisy engine. James slammed the door shut, since he was the last to get out and it hadn't shut the first time. "Hey, Charles, it's about time the folks bought you another car, isn't it? This one's getting a bit worn."

"I'll talk to them about it next time I go home for a visit," Charles said while standing in front of the quiet building.

"Are you sure this is the place?" Henry asked.

"Sure," Charles said. "Pete should know where his own club is. What did you expect, neon signs flashing 'Speakeasy' for three blocks?"

"No, I suppose you have a point there," Henry said and reached to knock on the door.

"Does Pete really own this place?" James questioned in disbelief.

"You evidently haven't heard the latest. He borrowed a wad of dough from some big shot to finance it. He thinks it's going to be big business. He's even dropped out of college."

The small, square, glass opening behind the iron grill swung wide and half a face and one eye peered through as a deep voice said, "who you looking for?"

"Peter Pan," replied Charles.

The glass square shut, and the door opened to reveal a huge man who resembled a grizzly bear in sight and smell as they passed by him to enter a small room with another door some ten feet away.

"It's through there and down the stairs," the bear-like man said.

The threesome started down the stairs.

"By the way," James said, "ask Daddy for a self-starter in the new, closed car, will you, Charles?"

"Sure. Why not?"

Charles headed straight to a white linen-covered table where Pete sat in a black tuxedo with shiny satin lapels. Charles led and James trailed behind Henry, looking about to take in as much as possible.

Charles shook Pete's hand. "Pete, you remember my friends, don't you?"

"Sure Henry, he said while shaking his hand. He then quickly withdrew it when he recognized James. "So you brought funny man, too." He stared at James distastefully.

"So you don't have a sense of humor. At least you have good taste in décor." James shrugged his shoulder as he looked around.

"Pretty nice, isn't it?" Pete said, waving his arm to draw attention to the surroundings. "Sit. The first drink is on me, fellas."

James couldn't believe the beautiful women who sat at the various tables. Some were accompanied by gentlemen, some were not. They drank and smoked as if women had always done so.

The mirrors about the walls made the establishment appear elegant and about twice its true size. He also noted that the band played well. "I'm impressed."

"And well you should be," Pete shot back. "I need a couple of partners. Any of you interested?"

"Yeah, I might be," said James.

"Sure," said Charles. "But why do you need partners? It appears you're doing well."

"Yeah, that's the trouble. The payments keep going up, if you know what I mean. My financier wants a piece of the action since I'm doing so well. He gets really rough if he doesn't get his way. I prefer not to be tied into the guy if I have a choice." He paused and took a sip of his drink. "I figure if I can get enough dough to cash him out, the payments won't continue to eat away at the place. Besides, it'll keep the gorillas from breathing down my neck."

"Sounds reasonable. How much do you need?" asked Charles. "I'm sure my family would be interested in the investment. They like to diversify."

"We'll talk figures later," he said as he rose, ready to introduce the approaching three young women. "Hello, ladies," he said as he reached for the blonde's hand. "Let me introduce, Henry, Charles and James, college friends of mine."

James couldn't take his eyes off of the center gal. Her blue eyes glistened, caught by the light as she glanced towards him. Her golden blond hair was bobbed, as was fashionable now. The beads and sequins on her straight dress sparkled as she moved to say hello. He didn't care to look at the other two. He was thunderstruck.

"Would you care to dance?" he asked as he sprang to his feet, hoping she wouldn't reject his request.

"Yes, thank you," she said as she took his outstretched hand.

As the evening wore on, James grew more enchanted with this beautiful lady. He had been with many females before, but this one was different, he thought. They kept each other company all evening.

"Come on, Beth. We have to get going," said the other blond, whose name James had not caught.

"Okay, just a minute," she said as she turned to James. "Thank you for a wonderful evening."

Her eyes caught his and spoke of a deeper fondness than did her voice.

"When can I see you again?" he asked. He held tightly to her hand as she rose from her chair to leave.

"Tomorrow."

"Where? When?" James knew his excitement was evident and he didn't bother to mask it.

"At the Stewart Hall Library, on the steps, at one." She pulled her hand away and turned to catch up with her friends.

"Someone's smitten," Henry teased.

"Smitten hell, he's thunderstruck," said Pete.

James ignored their remarks and simply stared as her pale blue dress disappeared up the steps.

It was very late when James got in, but the excitement he felt still stirred within him. He knew he would not be able to sleep yet, so he sat at his desk to share with his mother his new experience.

19 May 1923, Early Morning

Dearest Mother,

I feel I must share with someone what I am feeling, and since you are not only my favorite person in the world but also my best friend, I had to write.

I have met the most wonderful girl this evening. You'd love her. She doesn't even smoke, like all her friends. Tomorrow I plan to take her on a canoe ride. I can't help but recall the stories of your fond memories of when father attempted to win your heart with the secluded canoe trips.

I plan to find out as much about her as possible tomorrow and will write soon to share it with you. I'm sure you'd like her, Mother.

Love,
James

Ask, and it shall
be given you;
seek, and ye shall find;
knock and it shall be opened unto you.

Matthew 7:7

Chapter Seven

Kelly could smell the soapy clean fragrance of Danny's hair as she kissed him on the top of his head. She wondered if this was to be Danny's turning point in life.

Kelly felt the huge knot inside her stomach getting larger and the aching of her head pounded as if it wanted to explode into a thousand pieces. She hoped she would feel better once they reached the park and relaxed on the lush green grass. A decision could not be made as long as her head pounded. The back of her neck ached, and her shoulder muscles grew painfully tight. Her mind swayed back and forth, like children playing on a teeter-totter, with all the facts she had been told. There must be a deciding factor somewhere, she thought, she simply couldn't find it among all the wasteful ramble of emotions and facts her mind had created.

"Jason, is this decision making you as upset as it is me?"

"It's really an enormous decision they're giving us to make, isn't it, sweetheart."

Somehow, he didn't sound as if he meant what he was saying, she thought.

They pulled the car into a parking space and walked across the street onto the lawn at the bottom of the hill. Their arms were loaded with basket, blanket, cooler, and toys. Kelly sat Danny down on the lawn and spread the blanket with Jason's help. She inhaled the sweet smell of freshly cut grass. Jason sat and played ball with Danny while Kelly prepared three sandwiches. Jason's favorite was salami and cheese with hot green peppers, Danny loved peanut butter and honey, and for herself she choose cheese. This would be their early afternoon dinner, and the dessert would wait until evening when they returned home. Kelly poured three glasses of lemonade. Everything was done in threes, she thought. How empty she would be if anything happened to Danny and there were no longer three of them.

"Here you go, sweetheart," she said as she delivered the sandwich into Danny's hands. He managed it fairly well, she thought, as she gave the salami sandwich to Jason while still watching Danny.

"Would it be such an awful fate for him to stay handicapped rather than take the chance of paralyzing him or losing him forever?" she said.

"Kelly, if you were in his place, would you want to stay on the periphery of life, having never known whether you might have become a normal child?"

"Would that be so awful?"

As he sighed he put his hand to his head and rubbed his eyes with his thumb and index fingers. He removed his hand and looked at her, "I don't want to grow old regretting only what I've never done, and I certainly don't want to grow old and regret never having given Danny a chance to be normal. And, I have a difficult time understanding how you can feel so differently about such a monumental decision."

She was very aware of his impatience by the tone of his voice. She felt like a child being scolded.

"Kelly, I won't allow you to take this chance from Danny. It's a gamble, true, but, hell, if you don't gamble you can't win."

"Jason, I realize you feel strongly about this, but is it necessary to swear?" Kelly had been taught by her father that there was always a better, more intelligent word to choose rather than a swear word.

"I'm sorry, Kelly. I know that offends you, but I want this for Danny. Status quo just won't do," he said with finality. He turned away as if dismissing her, as he so often did.

"I don't know. I'm so afraid of losing what we do have," she said pathetically.

Jason ignored her words and played little touch games with Danny through the remainder of supper. Danny loved the teasing and the attention. Jason began to chase him while both were in a crawling position because Danny moved faster and with more agility that way. When he did walk, it was like a newborn animal. He was very unsure of his footing, and most of the time, held onto anything nearby. Jason now pretended to be a lion. As he would catch Danny, the lion would devour his prey. Danny giggled with delight, so Jason growled even louder.

"Let's go see a real lion on the top of the hill," Jason said as he stopped to rest a moment.

Danny's eyes sparkled. "Lin, lin," he said as he bounced up and down in place.

Kelly quickly cleaned up the dinner scraps, and Jason helped her take the paraphernalia to the car.

As they boarded the zoo shuttle that went from the grassy picnic area to the top of the hill where the animals were, Kelly noticed the shuttle consisted of three boxcar-type vehicles, all attached to one another, with a little roof on the top and doors at the sides to keep people from falling as it rounded the corners of the steep hill. As she sat down she also noticed the seats were not padded, although the white molded plastic made them appear as though they were. The shuttle tugged slowly up the hill, and the guide welcomed the crowd to the zoo. She hoped Danny was as pleased and amazed with the sights and sounds as she was.

When the shuttle stopped, Jason put Danny on his shoulders so that Danny might have the best view possible. He did this often.

They walked up the ramp that went around a very large monkey cage and then down again. The monkeys didn't seem to be very active today. Then the three of them went down the path to watch the beautiful salmon-colored flamingoes in their shallow pond. Danny giggled as he pointed to the birds, which stood on only one leg at a time and walked as if in slow motion. They continued on to see the rest of the animals. Kelly's nostrils retracted as they encountered the odors from the elephants' area.

Kelly had momentarily forgotten her burden of deciding Danny's fate while they entertained him.

Several hours passed, and Kelly's stomach ached from cotton candy, pink popcorn, and cola. She was sure little Danny probably felt the same. It was getting late now and was time to leave.

Danny fell asleep on the way home, having had a full day for a four year old.

Kelly carefully changed Danny into his pajamas, trying not to wake him, even though he was much too tired to be awakened by a little movement. She tucked him under his covers and put his favorite baby blanket next to him so when he awoke in the morning it would be there for him.

It felt good to be home, she thought, as she undressed slowly and got into the shower. The warm water made her feel as though she were a sponge and could soak up all the water she could get. She stood and let the water pound onto her body for a very long time.

"Want some company in there?" Jason asked as he stuck his head through the door.

"I'm done. It's your turn." She hoped there would be plenty of hot water for Jason. She knew she had taken a very long shower. She slipped her pale blue, satin nightgown over her thin, creamy white body while Jason showered. The softness of the fabric felt good on her skin. She then brushed her thick, long, strawberry-blond hair one hundred strokes while Jason dried off.

It was still early, but it seemed like midnight instead of only ten. She could tell they were both mentally exhausted. Jason grew very quiet when he was tired, and he had hardly said a word on the way home.

Jason crawled into bed next to Kelly and put his arm around her. "I love you, darling."

"I love you, too. Are you still upset with me?" she asked timidly.

"No," he said, as he kissed her lightly on the forehead.

She knew this was his way of expressing how much he loved her. She held his arm tightly around her as she remained on her back looking at the ceiling.

"Jason, we need to discuss Danny's operation. What do you think? Have you come to any decisions?"

"You probably knew since early this morning what my decision would be, and, I guess, I made my feelings evident at the park today," he answered softly. "What have you decided?"

"I'm still uncertain about the operation, but I'm beginning to believe you're right about our purpose here. We must be put on earth for a specific reason, like all the beautiful animals with their many differences. I guess it's all balanced out. Danny must have his purpose, and I guess it's only right to give him every chance possible. I'll love him no matter how the operation turns out. It's in God's hands now." She turned and looked into Jason's deep brown eyes with love and stroked his soft brown hair at the temple. "Thank God, I have you. I love you so much, Jason. Thanks for being patient with me."

She lay there wondering if she actually made up her mind or if she was simply yielding to Jason's definite decision. One thing for sure, she thought, there was no question in Jason's mind as there was in her own.

Jason snored lightly. She turned her back towards him, and although her body and mind were exhausted, she knew it would be sometime before she found sleep. She would ponder Danny's fate for hours.

CHAPTER EIGHT

July 1923

James felt his life had taken a rosy turn. He paused as he sat at his desk and looked up and through the water-spotted window onto the park like setting. His desk faced the part of the campus that looked more like a park than any other area of the grounds. A large clean pond surrounded by six willow trees was to the right in the far distance. Several ducks lived nearby, and James could see them now, floating gracefully about the still, glassy water. To the far left were large tall trees that hung over a wide dirt path that led students from one doorway of knowledge to the next. The remainder of his picturesque escape was moist, green, lush grass. He could not see any students wandering about. His stomach growled. All the students must be having supper, he thought, as his gut growled its demands for food once more. His attention left the still-life picture in front of him as he concentrated on the more immediate need for fuel.

He knew he must jot off a short note to his mother before taking care of his personal needs, so he began to write.

15 July 1923

Dearest Mother,

I am truly sorry I haven't written in a while. I'm coming home in three weeks. I'll arrive Saturday afternoon, at 2:45 P.M., by train. I'm bringing someone special to meet you. I do hope you'll like her. See you soon.

Love,
James

The train ran swiftly along, pushing the scenery past at a rapid pace.

"Mr. Connectivich?" said an older, colored gentleman who worked for the railroad.

"Yes, I am he."

"I've been asked to give you a message, sir."

"Yes," said James anxiously.

He held a piece of paper up to his face and read:

"Your mother is ill and is unable to meet you at the station. She has arranged for a family friend to meet you."

"Is that the entire message?" asked James, wishing it were more explanatory.

"Yes, sir, that's all."

"Thank you. May I ask how you came by this message?" he asked quickly before the porter left.

"It was telegraphed ahead. We received the message at the last stop. We will arrive at your stop in about two and a half hours, sir."

"Thank you," he said as he handed the old fellow a few coins from his vest pocket.

"Thank you, sir," the porter said as he hurried along.

"What do you think is wrong with your mother?" Beth asked James.

"I don't know. I wasn't aware of any problems. She's never been ill in her life that I remember," he responded thoughtfully. He sat puzzled and stared out of the window, not seeing the passing landscape.

"Is there anything I can do?" Beth said, bringing him out of his daze.

"No. I'll be all right. I just can't imagine Mother being ill. It's very concerning."

It was a long two and a half hours before the train finally came to a stop. James watched the people standing on the platform to see if he recognized anyone. There stood an old man with a long white beard, hat and cane. James knew his mother had sent the neighbor, Mr. Joffrey, to fetch her son. James knew little of the neighbor since he had always been kept secluded from the world by his loving, but overly protective mother.

He stepped off the train before Beth, and turned to offer his hand for her assistance off the train. "Hello, Mr. Joffrey. It was very kind of you to come and provide transportation to my home."

"It is my pleasure to assist your mother if there's anything she needs." His voice crackled with age. He offered his hand to James, while looking at Beth.

"Oh, I'm sorry Mr. Joffrey. This is my friend, Beth."

"Nice to meet such a pretty lady," he responded.

They got into Mr. Joffrey's car. The remainder of the ride home, once off the train, didn't seem much shorter to James. The car came to a halt in front of the large stone house. James helped Beth from the vehicle, thanked Mr. Joffrey for the ride and hurried to the front door. Aunt Martha opened the door slowly. James felt impatient and wanted to help, but didn't. The double doors were made of thick solid oak and a beautiful clear leaded-glass panel, which increased the weight of the doors. The gray-headed, short lady reached up to hug her nephew.

"How is she?" James said impatiently.

"James, you look tired and worried. Your mother will be fine." Her tone was not reassuring.

"Aunt Martha, what's wrong? She's never been sick a day in her life."

"Come, come, James. It's only a bad cold. She'll be all right, sweetheart," She glanced over to Beth who stood behind James. "This must be your special friend."

"Yes, excuse me. This is Beth." He grabbed for her hand. "And this is my dear Aunt Martha.

She took the young woman's outstretched hand from James in both her wrinkled but warm hands, patting it gently. "I'm delighted to meet you, dear. We know how special you are to James." She turned to James "Go, dear. Go see your mother. I'll take Beth to her room, and we'll be up shortly."

"Yes, Aunt Martha," he said. He kissed her on the cheek, and scurried up the stairway, barely touching the polished mahogany railing.

He knocked lightly on the door and began to enter just enough to peek around the door. "Mother? Are you awake?" he said softly.

"Yes, dear. Come in, please." Her arms were held open for her son's welcome as she sat up in bed.

"I've been so worried, Mother. What is the matter?" He sat next to her on the lace spread.

"Darling, it's only a cold. Don't worry so. I'll be better soon." She spoke through a stuffed nasal passage. Her white embroidered handkerchief was conveniently wadded in her hand. She leaned back on the pillows propped against the huge oak headboard of the bed. Her long, golden-brown-and-gray hair hung down the left side of her breast. The ruffles of her gown clung to her

long smooth neck. She was still a very beautiful woman at her age, thought James. Her green eyes stared at her only child with love and concern.

"James, dear, I'll be fine. Now, go get your special friend. I'm very anxious to meet her."

"Mother, promise me you'll get well as soon as humanly possible," he said with sadness in his voice.

"Don't be silly. Of course I will, darling. Besides, you have Beth to worry about now." As she spoke they heard a slight knock on the bedroom door.

"Yes, come in." She strained to speak loudly.

The two women entered the room. James rose from his mother's bed. "Mother, this is Elizabeth McBay; this is my mother."

"It's a pleasure to meet you, dear. James speaks very highly of you in his letters."

"Thank you. It's a pleasure to meet you." She smiled at James and turned back to his mother. "James speaks of you constantly and with great love."

"I'm sure he did, but now he has you, my dear," she said sincerely.

Beth looked to James for help out of what seemed an awkward situation for both of them. James wasn't sure why his mother was talking like this. Surely, it couldn't be jealousy, he thought.

"Why can't I have both of you?" he asked his mother half-teasing.

"Be still, dear," she said in a slightly irritated tone of voice. She then turned to Martha. "Martha, please fix these two young people something to eat. I'm sure they must be hungry after the tedious journey."

James turned to Beth and Aunt Martha. "You two go ahead. I'll be down shortly," he said in a stern voice. He watched them leave the room and then turned to speak to his mother. She had rested her head on the fluffy pillows behind her and closed her eyes.

"Mother," James said softly.

Without opening her eyes, she said, "I'm tired, dear. We'll talk more later. Go to Beth, now."

"Yes, Mother." His heart ached, and tears puddle in the corner of his eyes. What on earth was wrong with her? Had she given up over a cold? Was it something he had done, or could this all be over Beth? No, he thought, that is too absurd. He was in a daze of puzzlement as he left the room.

That evening was a quiet one. James and Beth told Aunt Martha all about the college and the town they shared. They insisted she and James's mother come to visit soon.

He retired reluctantly, since he had not had another chance to speak to his mother and would have to wait until early the next morning.

"James, James, come quickly." Aunt Martha tugged at his shoulder. "Your mother wishes to speak with you."

He glanced at the clock near his bed. "Now?" he said, still half-asleep. "Why now? It's in the middle of the night!" He felt fear creep into his being.

"That's not important. You must hurry."

He grabbed his satin brocade bathrobe and hurriedly put it around him, searching for the armholes and his slippers at the same time.

Martha hurried ahead. She had to keep the fire going and the room warm.

"Mother," James said as he rushed to her bedside.

"James, darling, I've just had a marvelous dream, and I felt the need to share it with you."

James felt relieved.

"Your father appeared in the dream and called me to his side," she said joyfully.

Fear again entered James' being.

"Mother, don't talk like that." He backed away. "I won't hear of such nonsense. I thought this was only a cold you have."

"James, please try to understand. I want to go. I want to be with your father just as you now have Beth to be with you." She stared at him, waiting for a response. "Please, dear, come close." She held out her hand to him.

He slowly reached for it and took hold. It was warm, and her grasp was gentle.

"I give you and Beth my blessing, and I ask in return for your blessing to release me from this world to one in which I will be with your father after such a very long time." Her voice was still strong, and there was no concrete evidence of a very ill woman in the body that lay in the bed.

"Mother, don't be ridiculous. You only have a cold. I won't allow you to talk this way," he said frantically.

"James, there is no point in lying anymore. I have been ill for quite sometime. It's not only a cold. I also have cancer." She bowed her head. "I am sorry we didn't tell you sooner, but I didn't want you to worry."

"Mother, I won't let you go. There is talk of freezing the human body and containing it in suspended animation until cures are found. I won't let you go." His voice grew more frantic. He clung to her soft, warm hand as a tear

rolled down his cheek and into the corner of his mouth. He ran his tongue across his lip and tasted the salt. "Mother, you can't go," he said softly through the tears.

"James, dear, please come sit next to me. You have Beth now, you don't need me any longer. James, I have no desire to be here now or in the future. I wish to be with God and with your father." She eased him down next to her upon the soft mattress. "I know you don't understand, but someday you will. Promise me you'll love Beth as much as I know you've loved me and have many children to fill the large hallways of this house." She strained to reach his face in an effort to wipe away the tears with the embroidered handkerchief.

"Yes, Mother, if that is your wish." He looked into her green eyes and saw loneliness within. He wondered if his love for Beth had had anything to do with the rapid decline of her health. "Mother, have I done this to you?"

"No, my darling. Everyone needs someone, and now you have Beth. Be happy, my dearest child. Our time is at an end, but your and Beth's time has only begun."

"Yes, Mother." He no longer concentrated on her words. He wanted to stop the clock at this moment and never let go of his beloved mother, the only parent he'd known for most of his life. How could this be, he thought? I came home with happy news, and it's turned into a nightmare.

She closed her eyes peacefully as if to rest. She never again woke to this world. James sat by her side and held onto her hand for sometime, not willing to accept the fact she was no longer with him. The world would never be the same without his beloved Mother in it, he thought.

James and Beth stayed long enough to take care of the arrangements.

On the train ride home, as James watched the landscape zoom past into a blur, he swore to himself he would go into medicine to save people's lives. Those he could not save he would freeze until a cure was found. No one would ever have to give up a loved one again, not if he could prevent it.

The eye seems to demand a horizon.
We are never tired (or unhappy) so long as we can
See far enough.

Ralph Waldo Emerson

CHAPTER NINE

The operation was to take place in the most advanced hospital in the country. They were to fly to Dallas, Texas, to meet Dr. Hess at the Children's Hospital the following week.

Dr. Hess had used this hospital only for his high-risk cases because of its extremely advanced equipment. He was also a member of the board of directors there, although he spent a minimal amount of time in Dallas unless he had a particular patient there. San Francisco had been his home for some time now.

Kelly knew Jason was comfortable with his decision. She was not as certain as he, so she prayed daily that they were making the right decision. The week passed quickly as both Jason and Kelly looked forward to what they hoped would be a turning point in Danny's life.

Danny sat in his room on his musical rocking chair with his little brown teddy bear on his lap. He watched his mother closely as she packed his Mickey Mouse pajamas, red plaid robe, and brown leather slippers with the fur inside. She stopped for a second in thought as she noticed Danny and then walked over to him and knelt down. "Danny, are you afraid to go to the hospital?"

Danny shook his head from side to side as he looked down at his teddy bear.

"You know Dr. Hess wouldn't let anything happen to you, don't you? Mommy and Daddy will be there all the time." She lifted his somber little head up with her hand under his chin to look into his eyes. "Danny, I love you, and I would never let anyone hurt you." She gave him a kiss on the forehead and held him close as if to comfort any fears he could not express to her. She silently prayed Danny would come out of this brain operation a normal little boy. She whispered with her eyes closed and Danny's tiny head snuggled next to her heart. "Please, dear God, release this tiny soul from captivity."

She heard the sound of a car door shut outside. She knew it must be Jason home from work. He had asked for a four-week, leave of absence to be with his son during the crucial period. The other attorneys in the firm were happy to help out and take his caseload for the month.

"Come on. Let's go see Daddy," she said, as she held her hand out waiting for Danny to take hold. He didn't, so she picked him up and cuddled him in her arms.

At the door Jason put down his briefcase and reached out towards Danny.

"There's Daddy's boy," he said as he grabbed him up from Kelly and gave him a big hug. "How's my son?"

"No hos..." Danny obviously tried his best to tell his Daddy he didn't want to go to the hospital.

"Ah, come on. That's not my big boy talking. Mommy and Daddy will be there with you all the time. Mommy will get your suitcase, and we'll go for an airplane ride. When we get there, we'll all go check out the room you'll be in to make sure they're going to take good care of Daniel Ashley, okay?"

Danny nodded his head, but stayed snuggled in his Daddy's big strong, safe arms.

Kelly watched and could tell how frightened Danny was by the tight grip he had around Jason's neck. He was usually never this timid and dismayed. He had been around many doctors in the four short years of his life and had grown used to them, but had never stayed anywhere any length of time as a patient.

"Jason, are you sure this is the right decision?" she asked as they headed toward the airport.

He paused, looked straight at Kelly, shook his head side to side, rolled his eyes, sighed and said in an angry tone, "you bet I am. I'm just sorry you aren't as sure as I am."

"So am I," she responded in an almost apologetic tone.

The three and a half hour airplane ride was uneventful, but the taxi ride was not. The taxi driver had driven recklessly, swerving in and out of traffic. It was probably necessary to get out of the large airport, but it didn't do much for Kelly's nerves. Danny patiently sat on his mother's lap, watching all that was going on around him. There were horns honking, airplanes flying above, and people rushing along the sidewalks. The whole town seemed to be in a hurry to get somewhere.

Jason paid for the taxi, lifted the suitcases, and walked behind Kelly and Danny as the doors swept open with the electric eye peering down on all who entered.

Kelly first noticed that the reception desk was a large, round, massive object which occupied one-third of the room. The carpet was a bright, cheerful, orange tweed with thick padding. Pale yellow chairs were scattered in a comfortable manner around the room. Not the most up-to-date colors, Kelly thought, but cheerful. Almost immediately, a young gentlemen approached, with a tag pinned to his shirt that read Volunteer.

"My name is Bob. May I be of help this afternoon?"

Jason set down the suitcases. "Yes. We are here to have our son, Daniel Ashley, admitted for surgery."

"Please come this way, Mr. and Mrs. Ashley. May I help you with those suitcases, sir?" he said, as he reached for them.

"Yes, thank you." Jason seemed tired and grateful.

They followed him down the white corridor to a small room, overcrowded with furniture. Bob motioned for them to enter, and set the suitcases down. "I'll be back in a few moments," he said and turned to leave.

There sat a middle-aged, unkempt, blond woman who immediately appeared out of character for a hospital. Her perfume, which filled the room, was strong and offensive. She said little and what she did say had attitude. She flung items on the desk around as if angry, then with her nose towards the ceiling, she turned to look their way. It was clear she didn't want to be here. Kelly hadn't worked for many years now, but she instinctively knew this was not a happy or desirable employee.

"Have a seat." No friendliness entered her tone of voice. "Have you taken care of the admitting paperwork before arriving at the hospital?"

"Yes. We've filled out every form invented," Jason replied.

Kelly knew he didn't mean to be pert with the lady, but her attitude seemed contagious to all those around her. Maybe her perfume offended him as well, she thought with a smile.

"If you could sign these forms, I have in front of me, and then I will call one of our volunteers to escort you to your room," she said.

Bob appeared in the doorway with a smile. Kelly smiled in return. At least, he was a refreshing sight, she thought, as she rose from the chair to follow him.

Bob reached over the desk to take the paperwork from the admitting clerk. "All right little man, let's go see what your room is like."

Jason reached for the suitcases.

"Oh, no, sir. Please allow me to take those for you."

"How nice," Kelly said.

"Thank you, Bob," Jason replied, grateful for the help. Jason bent down to pick up Danny.

Bob led them down the hallway to the four elevators, which faced each other. They gave an appearance of dark, rich wood, which gave off a feeling of warmth. He turned and touched Danny's arm with gentleness.

"Would you like to ride on my chariot, little fellow?"

Danny smiled timidly, clearly recognizing that Bob's soft touch and friendly smile meant no harm to him.

The elevator opened to expose the cold, clinical, stainless-steel walls. There were doors at both ends of this elevator as if it had hidden passageways somewhere. It stopped at the fifth floor. Bob set the luggage down, bowed at the waist, and held his hand out in a forward motion.

"This is it, ladies and gentlemen." His lighthearted humor was refreshing, to say the least. After the Ashley's had passed, he hurried to grab the luggage and continue to escort them down the hall. "I'm sure you'll enjoy your accommodations." He opened the door to his left. "Here it is, the Marque de Hospital."

Both Kelly and Jason were impressed by what they saw. Kelly noticed the far wall was completely windowed with a complex design of wrought-iron a foot in front of it. In front of it stood a small, blue velvet love seat with a large vase of colorful silk flowers next to it. She had never seen such a well-decorated hospital room, she thought. The walls were soft, antique white, the carpet was short-knit, gray-and-blue sculptured tweed. To the right stood a large mahogany dresser and a matching wardrobe closet. The design of the furniture gave the feeling of being antique, but the condition of the wood had the appearance of being new. The bed was directly opposite with a light blue velvet bedspread. She walked over to the bed and ran her hand over the soft, thick nap of the velvet. "This room looks like it belongs in a plush hotel, rather than a hospital," she said to Jason. "Such pretty colors."

"Yes, it's very nice," Jason said as he continued to survey the surroundings.

"I trust you will be comfortable here for a while. Now, we'll go see the little fellow's room. It's just across the hall." Bob set the luggage down inside the door, then turned to lead the way once again.

The large golden brass numbers on the door read 505 for Danny's room. Kelly liked the number of the room because she had a feeling that five was a lucky number for her. She opened the door and was again impressed by the décor. The walls were covered with bright orange poppies with brown centers and beautifully bright green leaves all about. The poppies jumped out at her as she walked into the room, but in a friendly way, as if to hug her in a welcoming gesture. The Berber carpet was brown-and-beige tweed and the curtains matched. The hospital bed seemed equally as friendly with its bright orange covering. No baby stuff, she thought, just bright and cheerful. Kelly was pleased and less anxious for Danny's sake.

"Look at the pretty orange flowers, sweetheart," Kelly said pointing to them. Danny cuddled closer into her arms.

When they were inside, Bob set Danny's small suitcase near the closet. "This is Danny's closet and his washroom is right next to it." He opened the door for a short moment and then shut it. "The dining room is on the second floor and is open twenty-four hours for your convenience. Everything will be set up on a computer, so you needn't worry about any charges or other small matters while you're here. If you need anything at all, please ring for a nurse or orderly, as our staff is more than ample. It has been a pleasure, and I hope to be of service again soon." He shook hands with Jason, smiled at Kelly, and turned to leave.

"It's been our pleasure, Bob," Jason said quickly before Bob had left the room. Jason sighed deeply. "Well, he was pleasant, wasn't he?"

"Much better than our first encounter." Kelly grinned. "It's getting late. Let's get Danny in his pajamas."

"Come on, big boy." Jason took Danny, undressed him, and slipped his pajamas on him.

Using the remote control, Kelly turned on the television perched high above them. Danny was greatly entertained by the activity on television. He sat spellbound, as always, after he was tucked in.

"Mommy and Daddy are going across the hall to our room. We'll leave the doors open so you can see us, and we'll be right back." Kelly kissed him on the cheek.

Danny didn't seem to notice their exit. No wonder people had always referred to the television set as a babysitter, she thought, as she headed toward her room.

After they had put away their belongings, and peeked in to make sure Danny was still occupied, they walked down to the nurses' station only a short distance away.

"Has Dr. Hess been in yet?" asked Jason.

"He should be in shortly, Mr. Ashley. I saw you come in earlier and let his office know you had arrived. Is Danny all settled in?" the nurse asked.

She spoke to Jason as if she had known him for a long time, thought Kelly.

"Yes, he is," Jason replied.

A young woman with blond hair and blue eyes approached. "Excuse me, I am Patty, and I'll be one of Danny's nurses. I hope everything is satisfactory."

"Yes, everything is fine."

"We'll be serving Danny his dinner within fifteen minutes. Meanwhile, why don't you and Mrs. Ashley go get a bite to eat. You must be tired from your long trip. I won't let the doctor miss you, and I did want to get acquainted with Danny."

"Thank you, Patty. That's a good idea." Jason took Kelly's hand. "Doesn't that sound like a good idea, sweetheart?"

"Yes, but, Jason, let's not be gone too long. I'd like to stay with Danny until he goes to sleep."

"Sure." He put his arm around her as they walked down the hall.

Once they had eaten they returned to Danny's room to find Dr. Hess sitting on the bed watching television with Danny.

"Well, good evening," Dr. Hess said as he rose to his feet to greet them. He laid his hand on Jason's left shoulder. "Danny ate a very light dinner in preparation for surgery tomorrow morning. We will prepare him after he has been given a mild sedative. You will be given a wake-up call at five-thirty so you can be here when Danny is awakened. The anesthesiologist will talk to you then, and I will also see you before the surgery. We'll see you in the morning." He then patted Jason's arm, turned to say goodnight to Danny, and left with his normal confident stride.

Kelly and Jason sat with Danny until he was almost asleep. Kelly kissed his forehead. "It's time to go to sleep, sweetheart. We'll see you in the morning."

Jason tucked the blankets around his son and made sure Danny's teddy bear was covered as well. He kissed Danny's head. "Sleep tight. Daddy loves you, big fellow."

Kelly turned off the television and pulled up the metal sides of the bed to protect her sweet baby. She reached for Jason's hand and left the room, leaving the door open. "I do hope we have made the right decision for Danny," Kelly said as she walked over to the wall of glass in their room. She folded her arms in front of her and stared at the outside setting.

Jason walked up behind her and put his arms around her. "Of course it's the right decision."

"If only I had the faith you have in all of this."

"It'll be all right, you'll see. Everything happens for a reason." He released her and turned to switch on the television.

It was only eight o'clock, but they were both exhausted. They would watch television for a while and retire early. They knew tomorrow would be even more emotionally exhausting.

CHAPTER TEN

In September, 1923, James entered medical school. He found it extremely demanding and became involved in many different fields of medicine. The time passed quickly, and his deep involvement helped to keep his mind from concentrating on the loss of his mother. His choice of general practice was influenced by his desire to one day return to his small hometown. His choice in the scientific field of cryogenics was brought on by the desire to never again lose a loved one. Daily, this desire grew and would one day be an obsession.

James felt the painful emptiness in his heart from the death of his mother. It was Beth who had become his world now, and he loved her dearly. He vowed to himself that he would never willingly let go of his new treasure without one hell of a fight. The thought of immortality was becoming an all-consuming purpose in his work. He was determined to spend whatever time and energy it took to obtain such a fantastic dream. In 1924, James made Beth his wife. Although he knew it would be rough going for a while during his schooling, he was also aware that Beth was willing to allow him whatever time and devotion to medicine needed for him to obtain his goals.

They had a large wedding with Pete as best man, and the reception was held at Pete's huge new club. James and Pete had long since forgotten their differences and become good friends. The fact that James had invested a large sum of money in the club when Pete had needed it provided a bond that would endure.

Although, James had recently recovered his investment, it had not been voluntarily. James considered Pete as big time now, but Pete's partners didn't feel the same. Pete had insisted he find a way to pay his friends back, but it cost Pete more than anyone was aware. Pete wanted his friends safe from the tyranny that his racketeering partners submitted him too.

James and Beth spent two weeks in New York on their honeymoon in an exquisitely plush apartment, compliments of Pete. James felt it was time to write the appropriate thank-you letters. He sat at his desk and wondered how to go about thanking Pete for being so very generous. James could have well afforded the wedding reception and hotel accommodations in New York had he wanted to, but he was extremely protective of the inheritance his mother had left him. The largest part of the estate was handled by a well-known investment company. He felt Pete's generosity was extreme and wasn't sure how to go about thanking him. Maybe it would be easier to start the thank-you letters with Aunt Martha, he thought, and began to write.

27 June 1924

Dear Aunt Martha

We arrived home only yesterday. We couldn't wait to write and express to you how much we enjoyed having you with us for the wedding. We enjoyed your company so very much and hope you will come again soon.

We had a most exquisite time in New York. The sights took days to see, but we did indeed take time to rest and enjoy the time away from the studies and work.

Thank you for the beautiful silver tea set. I'm afraid right now it is a bit beyond our needs, but I'm sure one day Beth will make good use of it.

We send our undying love and will write again soon.

With all our love,
James and Beth

He and Beth would spend several hours writing letters such as these. The months passed quickly and summer was nearly over.

"James, we received a letter from a Mr. Asher, today," Beth said, as she handed it to him.

He unfolded the sturdy vanilla-colored stationery. He glanced at the letterhead; Westcott and Asher, Financial Managers and Advisers.

Beth read over his shoulder as he began to read. "Is that the company that handles your inheritance?"

"Yes." He continued to read.

2 September 1929

Dear Mr. Connectivich

I am hesitant to inform you of our concern regarding your late mother's estate and the stocks she held, but we feel we have no other alternative. The stock market seems rather unstable at this point, and we must be advised at once of what course of action you wish us to take.

We are aware it has been difficult for you to meet with our firm in the past, but we consider this of the utmost importance.

Sincerely,
Mr. Asher

He put down the letter and looked up at Beth. "What do you think?"

"James, you can't possibly take the time to go speak to these gentlemen. Your research studies would suffer if you were to leave for any length of time."

He realized he had made special efforts to impress on Beth how important his studies were in this last year of school. Being on the research team was paramount to his future plans in medicine.

"You're right," he replied. Besides, I haven't paid the slightest attention to the stock market or the investments since I joined the research team. I wouldn't be able to advise them of anything." He paused while looking at the letter. "I'll write them back." He rose from his chair and went to his desk.

9 September 1929

Dear Mr. Asher

You have always handled my mother's affairs in the most prudent way. I cannot possibly meet with you at this time. Please do as you see fit and keep me informed. I have great faith in your judgment.

Sincerely,
James Connectivich

The subject of investments was not discussed between them the matter was dropped. James knew his studies were at a critical point and diligently went back to his studies.

It was only a few weeks when James received another letter from Mr. Asher.

4 October 1929

Dear Mr. Connectivich

Thank you for you trust and faith in us. The market has again rebounded. We are proud that our foresight has been of good fortune for you.

When I last wrote to you and received your response, we bought several new stocks and thus added to the ones already held.

I think this shall put you in a very good financial position shortly. I will be sending you a formal accounting of the transactions in the near future.

Sincerely,
Mr. Asher

James filed the letter away and continued to focus his efforts and energy on his work as the weeks passed. He was grateful the money for his schooling was in no one's hands but his own. He also appreciated the fact that he was not responsible for handling the remainder of the funds at this point, since he didn't have the time or desire to get involved in it. He knew that schooling had been paid for regardless of what the stock market decided to do.

The weeks passed quickly, and he looked forward to the day when he and Beth could start a family. He envisioned his children running up and down the halls of his ancestral home that one day soon he and Beth would go back to.

"James, darling, we received a distressing letter today. You had better sit down to read it," Beth said.

"Is it that bad?" he asked, tired from classes and bothered by her urgency.

"I'm afraid so," she said.

James walked over to his desk, pulled out the chair and sat to read the letter Beth had handed him.

10 November 1929

Dear Mr. Connectivich

It is with my deepest regret that I must inform you that all assets your family placed with this firm have been lost in the fall of the stock market.

It has been my understanding that Mrs. Martha Mayfield has been residing in the home for many years, and taking care of the residence while you attended medical school. I am sorry to inform you that the bank will be asking Mrs. Martha Mayfield to vacate within two weeks. Perhaps you would like to inform her of these unfortunate circumstances yourself.

Please be informed that this firm is extremely distressed that such events have occurred thereby making it necessary to take such drastic and undesirable actions.

Sincerely,
Mr. Asher

James folded the letter and threw it upon the desk. "Short and sweet, isn't it?" He looked at Beth. "I guess I should have paid more attention to the stock market, and our investments."

"What happens now?" she asked as she knelt down and put her hands on his knees.

"I'll send a telegram to Aunt Martha and ask her to come stay with us."

"Good, I'd love to have her here," she said as she laid her head on her hands. She looked up again. "What about the property and the house? Doesn't that upset you?"

He stood up and walked over to the window, gazing out for some time before answering. "Yes, but I'll not commit suicide over them like so many other fools. It's only material objects and can one day be replaced. It's Aunt Martha who worries me. She can't be replaced, and she won't take this lightly. Anyway, when you're down, there's no place to go but up." He turned to Beth who stood by his side and stroked her soft, golden blond hair. "Everything will work out, Beth. It always does."

The two weeks had passed and James had wired the request for Aunt Martha to come stay with them three separate times. He was beginning to worry. He was tired from the pandemonium the stock market had created in everyone's lives, and he was mentally and emotionally exhausted by the intense work he had been involved in during the last two years of additional schooling. As he entered the door of their small apartment, he felt relieved to shut the door behind him, closing out the world.

"I'm home," he yelled at Beth who was not in sight.

She came out of the kitchen, her eyes and nose red. She was obviously upset.

"Beth, what on earth is wrong?" He could not remember ever seeing Beth as upset as she was now.

"James, sit down. I have more bad news."

"What now?" He sighed. He was not sure if he could or wanted to handle one more tragic occurrence.

"Aunt Martha has died." She began to cry again.

"Dear Jesus, how?" He stretched his hand over his eyes and waited for an answer.

"She refused to leave your mother's house. That's why we never got a reply from her." She paused but continued to cry.

He sensed there was more. "Go on."

"When the bank went to remove her, she set the house on fire. She swore they would never get their hands on the family's home. She died in the fire."

He removed his hand and stared at Beth for a moment, as if consuming the news she had shared with him.

"Good for Aunt Martha," he said as he attempted to take Beth in his arms in an effort to comfort her.

Beth stood back in amazement to look James eye to eye. "Aren't you upset?"

"Yes, darling, I'm upset, but what can I do? There are thousands of people who are going to have to start over and have lost loved ones in the process. I guess we're just one of those statistics now."

He cleared his throat in an effort to control his emotions, knowing he had to be the strong one in this terrible turn of circumstances.

"Yes, but Aunt Martha?" she said with disbelief in her voice. Beth turned away. "Oh, damn it. The world is such a mess."

James could tell she was angry. Beth never swore.

"Aunt Martha was eighty-one. At least she went out fighting. As for the house, we'll build another someday. It's silly to value items that can be replaced. Anyway, what else could I want?" In an effort to ease her sorrow he took Beth in his arms. "Besides, I'm already the luckiest man in the world."

"Why?" she asked innocently.

"I have you." He hugged her tight. "Where the hell's the gin Pete sent over last week? We could both use a drink." He wiped the tears from her cheek.

She pulled away. "It's in the cupboard with the dishes."

By the time she had followed him to the kitchen, he had downed one straight shot of gin and was mixing a drink for her.

"Thank you, James, but I really don't care for any."

"Okay," he said as he turned to her and grabbed her up in his arms once more. He held her so close that he became aware of their hearts beating, and the warmth from their bodies.

"There's no sense in being angry at the world, Beth. Things have to get better. Even if they don't for a while, we still have each other. We'll get through this."

"Yes, I know, James."

"You're all I have anymore, and I never want to lose you. Never." James stroked her hair at the temple once lightly.

"You'll never lose me, James. I'll be with you always." She pulled away and kissed him quickly.

"Beth, I'd like to start a family soon. We need to get on with life."

She patted the side of his face lightly with her soft hand. "Are you sure this is a good time to do that?"

"Sure. Life goes on," he said as he kissed her with a long, loving kiss.

All things are possible to him that believeth.

Mark 9:23

CHAPTER ELEVEN

The telephone sounded the morning wake-up call for Jason and Kelly. At 5:35 there was a knock on the door.

"I'll get it honey," Jason said to Kelly, who was in the bathroom. He opened the door. "Oh, breakfast. Thank you."

The young lady, a volunteer, brought in the tray, set it on the table, and quickly turned to leave.

He lifted the stainless-steel covers to find sausage, eggs, toast and orange juice.

"The room service here is better than at some hotels we've been in," he said, raising his voice so Kelly would hear over the sound of the running water.

"Smells good," she said as she came out of the bathroom. "But I couldn't eat a thing. My stomach feels like it's tied in knots."

Jason ate and hurried to get dressed. They both wanted to be there when Danny was awakened.

It was six o'clock as they quietly entered. The nurse was also about to enter. She had come to awaken Danny. Kelly leaned over to kiss his forehead and brush his thick brown hair from his angelic face. He looked so peaceful and so very normal while he slept, she thought.

Soon all that beautiful brown hair would be shaved off and gone. The loss of hair for a short time was but a small price to pay if the operation was successful. Successful. Oh, dear God, please be with Danny today, she thought as she stroked his hair.

"Good morning," another cheerful nurse said as she entered holding the shiny silver prep tray. On it laid the syringe that would return Danny to the sleep he had recently come from. Kelly knew it was about to begin, and the many hours she had spent wondering about the operation would now prove to be wasted hours as reality commenced.

"Excuse me, Mr. Ashley, maybe you could help Danny go to the bathroom for us before we give him the sedative?"

"Sure. Come on, big fellow." He lifted Danny from the bed and headed toward the bathroom.

Kelly felt as though she were detached from the script and was watching as an outsider. She glanced out the window as she waited for Danny to return while the nurse straightened the sheets. The sun was warm as it entered the window, and there were only one or two small clouds hanging gracefully in the sky. The lawn that surrounded the hospital was a deep, lush green, and it gave a feeling of serenity to the scene.

"It's going to be a good day, it appears," the nurse said to Kelly, bringing her back into the reality of what was happening.

"In every way, I hope," she replied as she turned from the moment's escape she had stolen.

The door opened, and Jason set Danny back on the bed.

"It's all taken care of, nurse."

"That's a good boy," Kelly said, as she again stroked Danny's thick hair.

"Good. Now Danny, I'm going to give you a shot to make you sleepy. You'll only feel a small pinch. Can you turn over on your left side for me, please?" the nurse said, poised to stick the little fellow.

The hospital personnel seemed to treat everyone the same. Although it appeared to be only a routine, everyday type of job with a paycheck for them at the end of the week, there had to be more to it, thought Kelly. She couldn't imagine anyone changing bed pans and sheets simply to make a living. There was definitely something special about people who devoted themselves to the service of other people day in and day out, even though they appeared unaffected by the daily happenings and different patients. Maybe they simply had to teach themselves to remain unattached to the patients and their particular circumstances in order to remain sane.

The nurse proceeded to give Danny his shot. He was very brave and acted as if he were well aware of what had to take place, Kelly thought.

"Okay, it's all over sweetie. You can roll on your back now. I'll be back in a few minutes," she said as she glanced up at Kelly holding Danny's hand.

It was only a few minutes until Danny started to react to the sedative. His eyes began to close, and he tried hard to open them wide again.

"Danny, it's okay. You're going to sleep for a while, so you don't have to fight it. Mommy and Daddy will be right here, holding your hand. Don't worry, sweet man, we won't leave your side." Kelly's voice gave off a slight crackling sound as if she were about to cry, but she held it back. Be strong, she told herself. Be strong.

Danny smiled and let sleep overcome him.

A gentleman with sandy hair, green eyes, a rugged-looking face and wearing a white hospital jacket entered the room. "Mr. and Mrs. Ashley?" He held out his right hand toward Jason and then Kelly. "I'm Dr. Jack Baydon, your son's anesthesiologist. We will be giving Danny the normal dose of anesthesia to begin the operation, but as I'm sure Dr. Hess has discussed with you, we must reduce the anesthesia once the operation is underway and give him only enough anesthesia to keep him drowsy. He must be semiconscious for part of the operation, but there will be no pain whatsoever. We will use Mannitol to control both intracranial and blood pressure, and corticosteroid for the control of the brain's swelling after surgery." He paused, looked at Danny and then continued. "He will be taken directly to intensive care after surgery, at which time you will be notified and allowed to be with him." He handed them his business card from his left top pocket. "Here is my card for future reference. Are there any questions I can answer for you?"

"No, I think that covers it. Thank you, Doctor." Jason again shook his hand.

Two young men wheeled in a gurney of black leather with a wide, woven strap across the center of it.

"Good morning. We are going to take this little fellow down to the operating room. The doctor is probably down there if you want to talk to him. It's on the third floor."

Kelly watched one of the young men as he went about his duties. After checking Danny's wristband to be sure he was indeed Daniel Robert Ashley, he began the procedure of transferring Danny to the gurney with the help of his fellow orderly.

"Thank you, gentlemen," Jason said as he held his hand out to Kelly. "Come on, sweetheart. Danny is off in dreamland for a while,"

Kelly found it hard to pull herself away from her baby's side.

As they walked down the hall towards the nurse's station, Jason put his arm protectively around her shoulders once again. She still felt unsure. Dear God, please let Danny come out of this normal, she prayed silently.

Dr. Hess was talking with one of the nurses when they approached. He immediately excused himself from the conversation and walked to meet them. "Well, how's Danny this morning? I've been informed that he is resting and will be on his way down shortly."

"Yes, that's right," Jason replied.

"Good. We will shave his head while he's asleep, and he should wake up partially, shortly after that. The sedative is basically to relax all parts of the body and reduce any apprehension. The operation will take from four to six hours. You are welcome to wait in our waiting room across the hall from the operating room if you wish, but I believe you would be far more comfortable in your room. We will be in immediate contact with you if any complications should arise. However, I don't as yet foresee any."

He seemed so confident, thought Kelly, but she still felt unsure that they had made the correct decision. She interrupted her own thoughts with the idea that maybe she hadn't made the decision at all, and had only gone along with Jason's decision.

"Kelly, you appear to be a little upset," said Dr. Hess. "Is there anything I can do for you? Would you care to take something to calm you?"

"No, thank you, and yes, I am upset. That's my only baby you'll have in your hands this morning." Her voice quivered and tears welled up in the corners of her eyes. She used the tips of her fingers to wipe them away before they streamed down her face.

Jason put his arm around her and handed her his handkerchief.

"Is it clean?" She laughed through the tears. She knew her emotions had gotten the best of her again. She didn't know whether to laugh or cry; she only wished she felt better about this operation.

"It'll be all right, sweetheart," Jason said and then turned to Dr. Hess. "We'll be in our room. Thank you, Doctor."

She noticed that Jason's voice held a bit of apprehension also, now that the operation was close to beginning.

"Good. Good. We'll give you a call when Danny is out of the operation and taken to the intensive care unit for recovery. At that time, we'll discuss the outcome." He walked them partially down the hall. "Now try to relax. It's best for Danny if you're not tensed up when he wakes up. Everything will be fine." He then turned and left as abruptly as he had approached them.

Jason and Kelly entered the elevator hand in hand. It was amazing the sense of security she could derive from someone's warm touch, she thought.

Kelly was quiet, but her mind raced. She felt it would be easier to be the one facing this operation with its high degree of risk, rather than to watch her tiny, precious son submitted to such a perilous experience. I doubt that I would have the courage this tiny soul has, she thought. Maybe it was age and the life knowledge you acquired that built the fears within. Maybe it was simply that she really did have a lack of faith in everything that encompassed her world, as Jason had so often said so often. Her thoughts turned to Danny. He must have been born with the same faith and love of life Jason had always had. He was always such a happy child.

It was odd there was so little to say to each other at a time such as this, she thought as they entered their room, but the caress of a warm, loving hand seemed to convey the feeling of camaraderie to each who shared the burden. The next six hours would seem more like six days to them.

CHAPTER TWELVE

1934

The telephone rang. Beth answered it.

"It's for you, James," she said, handing him the phone.

"Hello"

"James, how the hell are you, ol boy?" asked the voice at the other end.

"Henry?"

"Yeah. How have you been? It's been a long time."

"Yes, it sure has. I'm fine how's the business world treating you?"

"Good. Really good." He paused "There's a specific reason for my calling, James." He paused again. "I heard from Pete the other day. He said he needed to talk to us. He's in some sort of trouble."

"Trouble? Did he say what it was?"

"No, he didn't but I suspect he's in over his head with that bootlegging gang he's tied to. I've heard rumors to that effect for sometime now."

"Okay. When does he want to talk to us?" asked James.

"He said next Tuesday afternoon at his mother's old house. Can you get away from the hospital?"

"Sure, Henry. I'll make it a point to get away." He answered, "I owe the guy that much."

"Great. There's only one problem." Henry said, and then paused.

James felt himself falling into a trap. "Yeah, what's that?"

"Neither Charles nor I can make it Tuesday. Charles is in Europe on some medical business, and I can't possibly leave town next week. I have big meetings, big deals coming down right now." Henry paused, apparently waiting for a response. There was none. "Could you possibly go talk to Pete and let me know what's going on?"

"Sure," he said reluctantly. He knew all three of them owed Pete for favors given them when Pete was on top. "That's the least I can do for Pete." He hoped Henry would get the message. He didn't.

"Thanks, James. I owe you one."

"Yeah, sure." A lot of good that would do him, he thought. It didn't seem to matter that Henry also owed Pete. "I'll call you when I get back from meeting with him."

"Thanks again, James."

James heard the click at the other end before he replaced his receiver.

"Who was that, dear?" asked Beth, who sat knitting a white baby sweater.

"Henry. He wants me to go talk to Pete on Tuesday. Pete's in some sort of trouble. I can't imagine why Pete didn't call me instead of Henry or Charles," he said, as he sat down and picked up his book to continue reading.

"Are you going? Can you get away from your work?" she asked while laying down her knitting.

"Yes, I feel obligated to go," he said and continued reading.

His briefness was clearly a sign he didn't want to discuss it further. He hoped Beth understood. He watched her pick up her knitting out of the corner of his eye, and knew she had gotten his nonverbal message.

He got out of the taxi, paid the driver, and headed for the porch. He noticed the dirty white porch swing hanging idle. How odd that Pete would choose his old home as the meeting place. Maybe his trouble was really serious, he thought as he reached for the handle on the rickety screen door. There was none. He looked through the screen and noticed the door had been left slightly ajar. He paused and looked around the yard. He didn't like the vacant feeling in his stomach. The smell of the dry ground filled his nostrils, and the silence filled his ears.

"Pete?" He opened the screen door cautiously. It creaked as he pulled it towards him. He knocked on the trim of the opened door. "Pete, are you in here?" he called loudly into the house. He approached slowly. Maybe he was in the basement. He recognized what sounded like a loud ticking. It was the old, pale green porcelain clock on the mantle. "Damn it, Pete," he murmured. "Pete" he called out loudly.

The dainty lace doilies graced the backs and arms of the sofa and chairs. As he looked about, he noticed the smell of kerosene sting his nostrils. He turned his attention toward the pale pink lamp sitting upon a heavy magahony table with a large, cold-looking slab of marble on top of it. Why would anyone burn a kerosene lamp during the day? he wondered.

"Pete," he said cautiously. His muscles at his shoulder blades tightened. Where the hell was he? James thought.

Then to the left of him, he saw a door ajar with a garment of clothing hanging on the knob. He noticed that it did not appear to have been carefully placed there, but looked as if it had gotten caught while someone passed by.

He approached slowly. He felt his adrenaline rise. He glanced into the room, and noticed the gleam on the brass bed from the sun shining against it. He reluctantly looked down at the disheveled bedcovers. He saw what looked like a figure beneath the white sheets and multicolored quilt. His glance continued over the sheets and stopped at the deep red spots coming through from the underside.

"Damn it, Pete, is that you?" He hurried to the side of the bed and lifted the corner of the sheet. "Shit." Pete had been shot several times in the stomach. Most of the blood had dried. He had evidently lain here for some time. "Sorry I didn't make it in time, pal," he said out loud.

He laid the sheet down and started for the telephone. His stomach felt nauseated as he spoke to the police about the death.

Then he dialed home. Beth answered.

"Darling, I won't be home until tomorrow."

"Why, James?"

"I didn't get here in time. Someone got to Pete," he said quietly.

"Oh no."

"See you tomorrow. Noon train, Beth."

"Be careful, James."

"Hell, sweetheart, no one would stick around after this. It's okay. I love you."

"I love you, too. See you tomorrow, James."

"Bye, sweetheart."

Beth met James at the train. "Are you all right? You look so tired and worn." She inserted her hand in his arm as they walked to the car.

He patted her hand upon his arm. "I'm better now that I'm home with you." He kissed her forehead and then opened the car door for her. He went to his side, got in and shut his door.

"James, sweetheart, I've kept a secret from you." She smiled and happiness sparkled in her eyes. "I know you're upset about Pete, but I have good news I think you'll like."

"Okay, I'm ready for good news right about now." He smiled back at her.

"I'm three months pregnant, sweetheart. I didn't tell you because I know how worried you'd be that I'd have another miscarriage. Are you excited?" she asked.

"Excited? You know I am. This time you'll go to bed and stay there. No arguments."

"Yes, sir." She leaned over, kissed him and sat back.

He touched her stomach. "I hope it's a boy."

After a few moments of silence, he said, "you know, Beth, it'll be awfully nice to see new life instead of so much death."

He had taken Pete's death hard. He hated to lose anyone he loved. He felt it was like losing a battle with immortality.

With men this is impossible;
But with God all things are possible.

Matthew 19:26

Chapter Thirteen

Dr. Hess dressed quickly in his green pants, shirt and paper cap. He then rushed from the locker room across the hall to the washroom outside the operating room where all neurological surgery was done because of the extensive equipment which filled the room. It was beyond imagination the money that had been spent on the most highly advanced technological machinery. The equipment in this room was known to be the best, and this hospital was considered the only place for the most challenging and unprecedented brain operations in all the country. Dr. Hess put on his mask, scrubbed his hands and hurried through the large stainless-steel swinging doors. Once his hands were dried, he held them out and was assisted with his first set of gloves by the nurse who patiently waited for him. He glanced at the machinery that lined the room. He took note that the cardioscope was normal and the team of assistants and nurses waited in readiness. The resident assistants had done all the preparatory work of placing Danny in the Mayfield head rest, while padding his shoulders, arms and legs with gel padding to reduce or avoid any pressure injuries. No incision could commence until the attending surgeon was in the room and the time out session had occurred between all persons in the room. "We're ready for you, Dr. Hess," said Bill, the chief resident."

Once the incision site was marked, Dr. Hess requested 1% lidocaine with epinephrine injection to prevent post-operative pain and to control the bleeding during the procedure. He held two lap sponges to dab the blood as he made the incision while Bill assisted with the suction tubing, keeping the site clear. The layers of the scalp once incised where held in place with the scalp clips, and then covered with a saline moistened lap sponge to keep the tissues from drying out during the long procedure.

"Drill." Dr. Hess was ready to place a burr hole in the skull which was required for the placement of the side-cutting craniotome to cut the skull for access to the soft tissues of the brain. Once the craniotomy flap was removed Dr. Hess handed it to Nancy, the surgical technician, to be wrapped in a sterile sponge soaked in antibiotic irrigation and safely stored on the back table.

"3-0," Dr. Hess said quietly. He was totally absorbed in what he had to do and knew that his team knew what the steps to this procedure were. He used the suture to tack the dura and pull it out of the way. He looked up occasionally to check the Brainlab screen for placement of instruments within the brain. Bill stood next to him ready with the bovie used to cauterize any bleeders.

"Large pattie," he reached for the 6 inch by 1 inch, white cotton strip with a blue string down the middle which provided for prevention of being left inside the patient. He used many of these cotton pads of varying sizes. They had been moistened by the tech to prevent them from sticking to the fragile tissues of the brain.

The huge, steel and LED lights threw a strong, shadowless, penetrating beam toward the area that was being worked on. The room was well lit, but it was time to turn almost all the lights off and bring in the microscope for the more detailed work.

"Let's bring T-rex in." Dr. Hess said as he backed away from the open wound.

Erica, the circulating nurse, pushed the huge microscope into the area that Dr. Hess had occupied a moment ago, being careful not to touch the plastic drape that had been put on T-rex a short time before for purposes of sterility.

"Jack, are you ready to wake the patient," he asked as he stepped back into the operative field.

"Sure, I'm ready when you are." Jack Baydon was the anesthesiologist that Dr. Hess had requested on his most difficult cases. They had worked together for many years and had created a special trust over the years.

"Ok, let's do it then." Dr. Hess waited for several moments while Danny regained semi-consciousness. "Danny, can you hear me?" No reply. He waited another couple of minutes.

"Danny, can you hear me?"

"Yes." His response was clear and sounded appropriate for a boy of four, rather than his normal one year old sound.

"I'm going to ask you to move parts of your body for me. Can you do that?"

Danny tried to move his head in a positive response, but the massive clamps held it motionless. "Yes."

Dr. Hess patted Danny on the shoulder lightly through the blue draping that keep the operating site sterile. He moved slightly to the side to view the angiograms and CAT-scans on the large 60 inch screen on the north wall of the room. It looked much like a road map, but helped the surgeon to chart his way into the regions of the brain that had been affected by the nature of the defective brain tissues. He would now use the tiny microscopic instrumentation to maneuver into the brain, while being careful not to move to quickly.

The room was quite. It was a rule of neurosurgery that when the patient was awake everyone in the room had to be quiet. The only sounds were those of the beeping anesthesia machine, which read the patient's pulse, blood pressure, and heart rate. In the silence the dedication was discernible as each participant directed all their efforts to help this small, vulnerable, defenseless little boy which lay on the table.

Nancy assisted the doctors with putting on a second set of gloves which were half a size larger to insure that all precautions would be taken against infection. Meanwhile the circulating nurse, who was not sterile, slipped a snugly fitted headlight onto the doctor's head without comprising anything that was sterile. He looked like a miner ready to descend into the mines.

"Danny, move your left foot." He did so. "Good. Now move the other foot." He did so. Dr. Hess touched an electrode to the tissues of the brain. "Can you feel anything, Danny."

"No," he replied.

"Danny, can you move your right hand." He moved the wrong hand, but Dr. Hess knew Danny wasn't familiar with left and right at this point in time, so he continued. "Can you move the other hand for me." He paused. "Can you move that same hand again?"

Dr. Hess was now at the base of the brain, near the thalamic region with a large area of the gray matter exposed for exploration with the electrode. He placed the electrode again. "Can you feel anything, Danny."

"Yes. My tummy."

"Does it hurt?"

"No."

"Does it feels like pins sticking you?"

"Yes."

"Danny, can you say good morning to Dr. Baydon?

"Good Morning," he spoke more clearly and more completely than he had ever done while awake and functioning normally.

"Great Job Danny. Now just relax for me little man."

Dr. Hess handed the electrode to Bill. "Hang on to this."

He took the knife and cut closer to the thalamus, which was sometimes spoken of as the soul itself; although it was only speculation on anyone's part how near the tumor was to the thalamus. He held his hand out again, and like clockwork, Bill laid the electrode into his hand. He applied it very deeply to the left, very near the corpus callosum.

"NO!" yelled a deep masculine voice. It was much older than that of a four year old, but it had come from Danny's lips.

"What the heck?" Bill's surprise was evident by his comment.

Dr. Hess quickly looked up to see who had just spoken. He shook his head in a scolding manner. Danny was still awake and quiet was the rule, and Bill should have known that. He returned to his work.

"Let's try that again." Dr. Hess said as he went about his work without any hesitation, almost as if he had expected what he had just heard. It was obvious that no one else in the room had ever experienced or expected such a result. The room was still and silent.

He proceeded to insert the electrode to the same point. All eyes turned toward Danny. Those on his right side watched the lips intently to be sure this was reality. As Dr. Hess held the electrode, Danny's body was still, but suddenly, as he touched the same gray matter again, the deep voice shouted, "No. No. Not Yet! Nooooo!"

Silence followed for a few seconds and then again in a screaming, masculine voice as if someone were in great danger, "No Dr. Connectivich God No," then the voice trailed off, "cooollldd." Silence.

Dr. Hess removed the electrode. "Jack, how are the vitals?"

"No change, not even during the speech." His voice sounded surprised as he spoke.

Danny was lying very still, obviously not realizing what was happening.

Every eye in the room turned to Dr. Hess, with questioning looks.

"Hmmmmn," was his only response, but it was evident his mind was moving a mile a minute taking in what had just occurred and working it out in medical terms.

"Jack, was Danny's body still and relaxed at all times during the voice response?"

"Yes, all but the face, which looked as if he was scared to death. He seems calm now, and the cardiograph registered no change at all during the occurrence of the voice."

"Hmmmn. Let's try it once more."

He placed the electrode. Nothing. No response at all. Dr. Hess moved the electrode slightly one way and then the other. Nothing. He paused a moment.

"Jack let's get him back to sleep." He waited several minutes before speaking again.

"Let's get the tumor out," he said as he handed the electrode to Bill. "Retractor."

Nancy responded. He placed large patties on the surface of the gray matter and gently placed the malleable black retractors on the side of each hemisphere. He paused and studied the large television screen on the wall to check where the Brainlab pointer was directing his path to the deepest regions of the brain. He had chosen to go down through the middle because he couldn't tell how far inward the tumor had grown and there was less chance of damaging the more useful part of the brain. There was no sign of the tumor yet. The progress was slow. The minutes ticked into hours. There was no room for mistakes this near the thalamus, since it was the region of the brain in which all sensory experience was processed before being transmitted to the cortex. The slightest mistake could create numerous ways in which Danny could be paralyzed for the rest of his life; or perhaps he would not last through the operation if a major artery were cut. The only reason such a deep tumor was considered operable was the young age of the patient. Only then would such an acute risk be taken. Years ago it would have only been considered a matter of time until the tumor grew and literally took over the brain.

"There's our baby. Spoon." He held out his hand without turning his head away from the microscope.

Nancy handed him a small, copper spoon used to scoop out the diseased growth. Bill was ready to assist with the micro-scissors in one hand and the bovie cautery tip in the other.

Dr. Hess struggled to reach the tumor. He had Bill cut and cauterize carefully as he separated and scooped slowly. They worked for several hours.

"Damn. I can't get all of it." He laid the spoon down on the tray to his left, stood back, and thought a minute. "It's too risky. Let's close it up."

"Okay Bob, that's it. Thanks Danny you did a great job, we'll been done in just a little while." He spoke as if Danny was semi-conscious although he was still under sedation.

"Okay Erica, you can get t-rex outta here please and turn the room lights on." She moved quickly, knowing how exhausting this type of operation was for the doctors.

Dr. Hess looked at the osteoplastic flap that had been prepared by the residents. "Good. Looks good, Bill."

Dr. Hess laid the dura over the grayish pink gelatinous mass as it pulsated gently inside the tiny skull, then fitted the skull to its previous location and prepared to complete the attachment to the rough edge of the skull. "Screw," he said as he held his hand out to receive the screw driver with the tiny screw at the end. He glanced up as Nancy placed the handle in the palm of his hand.

"Well, what do think?" Bill said to Dr. Hess.

"We'll discuss it after in the office." His reply was short and to the point. It was clear he didn't want to discuss it in the presence of the operating room staff. He tightened the last screw and laid down the screw driver on the mayo stand next to him.

"Bill do you mind doing the rest of the closure?"

"No, I'll be happy to."

Dr. Hess stepped back a few feet, pulled off his gloves while viewing the screen on the wall. He removed his gown, threw it in the large plastic trash bag and left the room. He went directly to the locker room and sank into a well-padded, worn green chair, exhausted. He picked up the telephone on the table next to the chair and pushed the buttons which started his dictation program.

"Opening began with incision, removal of osteoplastic flap, comma, dura mater removed and clipped, comma…"

CHAPTER FOURTEEN

1938

"Guess what I see, little Luke?" his mother said.

His large blue eyes turned her way. "What? What do you see?"

"Well, it's something you love very much, and it's half white and . . . well, that's enough clues. Come on. Guess before it's too late," she said, as she rocked slowly on the porch swing.

Luke put down his wooden train engine, turned his head to look over his left shoulder, and yelled, "Daddy. Daddy." He quickly bounced down three steps and headed for his Daddy with his arms wide open.

James stopped, knelt down, and held his arms wide for his little boy.

"Daddy. Daddy." Luke yelled again, just before flinging himself into his daddy's arms and against his chest.

The large adult arms closed rapidly around the fifty-three pounds of soft, loveable little boy. "How's my beautiful boy?"

"Did you bring me a surprise, Daddy? Did you?"

"Yes." He kissed his son on the forehead as Luke lowered his head to search the pocket of the doctor's white jacket for his surprise.

"Yum," he said as he pulled out a black shiny paper wrapper with his favorite candy, a licorice stick.

"Not until after dinner, little fellow," said his father.

He knelt slightly to set his son down. "Come on. Let's go see Mommy."

"I'll beat you, Daddy," Luke said as he took off running without waiting for an answer of acceptance.

James jogged to the porch, making sure his Little Luke was just a short distance ahead.

"Hurrah," called his mother from the porch.

Luke smiled up at his father while breathing hard. "I won again, didn't I, Daddy?"

"You sure did. Do you ever think I'll be fast enough to win?"

"Oh, someday," he said, trying to sound grown up. He then sat on the top step to catch his breath.

"Hello, Darling," said Beth. "How was your day?"

"Great," he said, as his eyes opened wider, like a kid at the candy counter. "A fellow named William Barry paid us a visit today down at the lab. He's a highly intelligent gentleman. We all got so excited discussing the new procedures being used in the preparation of the patient for storage that we neglected most of the day's work. By the way, I invited him for dinner tomorrow evening. I hope you don't mind?"

"No, not at all," she said. "Come sit next to me, sweetheart." She moved her basket, which held her embroidery thread for the cross-stitch sampler she had been working on.

"Thank you. I'd love to, but Luke and I have a date to go down to the fishing hole before dinner, don't we young man," he said, as he tossed Luke's longish, soft blond hair about with the tips of his fingers.

"Yes sir." He rose to take his father's hand.

"Go get the poles. I'll wait for you, okay?"

"Sure." He turned to run toward the garage.

While removing his doctor's jacket, James spoke to Beth. "I can't tell you how excited I am about this new work." He watched his son intently until he was out of sight and then turned his attention to his wife. "I'll never have to lose my loved ones again," he said as he reached for her busy hand. "Wouldn't it be fantastic if death were eliminated altogether? It's hard to believe they could freeze a human and wait until a cure is found and then return him unharmed to live, hopefully, forever." He paused. "Someday soon the day will come, you know."

She put down her embroidery work and surveyed the excited eyes of her husband as her watched her. "Will it, dear?" she said lovingly.

"Yes. We'll be together forever. Is that too long for you, my love?" he said teasingly.

"No. As a matter-of-fact, James, it's not long enough. As long as you don't mind the wrinkles that'll accumulate over time, eternity sounds good to me."

"Come on, Daddy," yelled Luke, waving his arm at his father.

"Gotta go. We'll bring back dinner." He headed off towards Luke.

"See you soon. Good luck," she yelled after them. She secretly hoped they wouldn't bring back any stinky fish, but she didn't have the heart to spoil their fun. She had grown fond of the concept of catch and release, since her boys fished as often as was possible. As she watched them go she knew she had never been happier than since they moved back to James's hometown. Once they were out of her sight, she continued with her work.

It is God's privilege to conceal things,
And the king's privilege to discover and invent.
You cannot understand the height of heaven,
The size of the earth, or all that goes on in the king's mind.

Proverbs 25: 2-3

Chapter Fifteen

The telephone rang. Kelly dashed to pick it up.

"Hello."

"Mrs. Ashley?"

"Yes, yes."

"Your son will be in the recovery room in approximately thirty minutes. You are welcome to come down and be with him if you like, but he'll sleep for two or three hours."

"Thank you. Thank you." She hung up the telephone and turned to Jason. "He's out, only he'll sleep for another couple of hours, they said."

"Well, let's go." He got up from the plush velvet love seat, grabbed her sweater from the chair by the window, bent down to shut off the television, and headed towards the door. She hadn't budged.

"Well, come on, Sweetheart. Why the hesitation?"

"I'm scared. What if things didn't go well?"

"Well, whatever happened, it's all history now. Everything went well, you'll see," he took her arm and aimed her out the door and down the hall, shutting the door behind them.

They reached the recovery room and entered slowly. It was dimly lit, and there were no windows in the room. It was a very relaxing darkness though, she thought. Almost like the atmosphere of a restaurant that plays soft, mellow music at dinner. Then her thoughts were interrupted by a female voice.

"Mr. and Mrs. Ashley, Danny is over here. The nurse pointed to the right-hand corner of the room.

There he lay, head wrapped in bright white, sterile bandages. His eyes were closed restfully, and his breathing was easy and normal. They stood at the end of his bed. Kelly took Jason's hand as she watched their precious little boy lying bravely beneath all the machines that monitored him.

"He'll sleep for a while yet," said the nurse, who was taking his vital signs every fifteen minutes. "The doctor should be here shortly."

"Thank you nurse," said Jason. He turned to Kelly. "Let's let Danny sleep and go outside and wait for Dr. Hess to come down." Jason followed Kelly out.

She was again in her own little daze. It had finally come to pass after all those tests and trips to the hospital. She would feel better when it all ended and they were all home.

Within the next fifteen minutes, Dr. Hess appeared at the end of the hall, headed in their direction. Jason and Kelly stood up, waiting anxiously for him to arrive on the spot in front of them and disclose the facts of Danny's operation. He was still dressed in his light green surgical garb and was still, as always, completely composed.

"The operation in itself went well, but unfortunately we could not get the entire tumor out."

Kelly sat down when she heard this. This was not what she was hoping to hear, and felt faint at the news.

"We did get about ninety percent, it was difficult to reach, as we knew it would be. We'll keep our fingers crossed that it won't grow back. I know that doesn't sound very promising, but we'll try using chemotherapy on the remainder of the tumor since it is at the base of the brain."

Kelly watched Jason as he stared intently into the doctor's eyes. "What are the chances it will grow back?" Jason's voice was monotone.

"I'm hoping it won't but I can't give any guarantees." He paused, and kept eye contact with Jason. "I know my answer lacks substance, but a tumor such as Danny's makes it difficult to predict what'll happen next. If you want to come to my office, we can discuss this in detail." He paused again. "Meanwhile, Kelly, you might want to stay with Danny, in case he wakes up."

It was not like Dr. Hess to exclude Kelly in anything he had to say. Kelly looked at Jason with questions written on her face.

"It's okay Sweetheart. Go ahead and stay with Danny. I'll be right back and I'll share all the particulars with you." He bent down to kiss her cheek and then left with the doctor.

They were well down the hall when Kelly decided to go keep vigil on Danny.

"Look, Jason, there was a bit more to the operation." Dr. Hess said as he continued to walk down the hall.

Jason stopped in his tracks and waited for Dr. Hess to stop. He waited for more to be said.

"I didn't think Kelly could handle it, so I'll tell you and let you decide how and when to share the information with her."

"Oh-kay." His eyes and ears saw and heard no other sound or movement than that which came from Dr. Hess's mouth.

"We don't usually discuss our personal beliefs with our patients or their families, but it's necessary in this case. I believe there's more to this than a brain tumor." Dr. Hess put his arm around Jason's shoulder and began walking again, towards the conference room, which he used as an office when speaking with patients and/or their families. "While I probed Danny's brain for the nervous system's reactions to the electrode, I touched a particular spot. A very strange, older, masculine voice shouted a doctor's name and the word *No* over and over. The last word we heard was the word *cold*."

Jason had stopped and again stared in disbelief.

"I know it's hard to believe, Jason. I've never heard of anything like it before either, but it happened."

They entered the conference room. The poignant smell of coffee left on the burner all day filled the room.

"Sit down please," he said as he pointed to a chair. "Would you like some coffee?"

"No. No thanks. What do you think all this means?"

"Well, I wouldn't think much of it except for the doctor's name, Dr. Connectivich. I read about a doctor with a name such as that, years ago. The gentleman was one of the pioneers of cryogenics and contributed an enormous amount to the science. It stuck with me because he lived in Connecticut. It seemed odd that his name would be so close to the state's name. It was a sort-of word association thing that went off in my mind when I heard Danny, or whoever, say the name during the operation."

"That's crazy, Dr. Hess. Do you think there's some connection?"

"Yes, Jason, I do. The name is old-world and just too coincidental. I'd like to look into it a little, with your permission."

"Well, sure, go ahead if you think it'll lead you to something."

"Jason, we've discussed my beliefs about Danny before. There's more than meets the eye with that little fellow. Everything in life isn't always black and white. Sometimes you have to read between the lines."

"Okay, but let's not take this thing too far," Jason added.

"What's too far? What's impossible? Anyway, Danny's life is worth the effort. He's different from other brain-damaged children. You've known that for some time now."

"Yes, I have. Do what you feel you should, but don't let Kelly know just yet. It'd scare the holy hell out of her. She has a tough time dealing with out-of-box thinking when it comes to her little boy. She's been through a lot with the little guy." He grew impatient with Dr. Hess. It scared him too.

"I'll let you know if anything turns up. I'll call you at the office if it's necessary to communicate about this." He paused. "Besides, Jason, you've expressed to me that you believe as I do. There's a reason for everything that happens and there are no coincidences. Right?"

"Yes."

"I'm relieved the incident is out in the open and pleased I have your consent to research this Connectivich thing."

"Okay," Jason said as he got up to leave. He took one last, long look at Dr. Hess. "Okay," he said again as he turned to leave.

As he continued down the hall, he did his best to regain his normal composure. Kelly had been through enough. There was no sense in worrying her more.

CHAPTER SIXTEEN

1950

"Is Luke awake yet, Beth?"

"I don't think he is," she replied. "Are you going to teach him to drive today as you promised?" She watched him lower his book once again and reach for his cup of lukewarm tea.

"A promise is a promise," he said before putting the pink china cup to his pursed lips.

"Do you regret making your promise?"

"No, not actually, but he's still a bit young, don't you think?" He sat the cup down slowly.

"James, if the boy were thirty-two, you'd claim he was too young. Admit it, dear. You hate seeing him grow up."

"Yes, I guess I do," he said pensively. "If I can't keep him young forever, I will at least do my best to be around forever to watch my children and grandchildren grow up." He raised his book again.

"James, I don't mind being around forever, but will I continue to age? Can you do anything about that?" she asked for the twentieth time in as many years.

"Dear sweet Beth. I will make sure there is something invented to keep you as beautiful as you are now before I will allow any scientist such as myself to bring you back into the breathing realm."

She laughed. "Thank you, dear."

"Good morning, Mother," Luke said as he kissed his mother on the cheek. "Good morning, Father."

"Good morning, Luke. Would you like some breakfast?" she said.

"No thank you. Father, can we go now?" He stood next to his father, anxious for an affirmative answer.

"Go where?" he said as he pretended to continue to read his book.

"Father, you know. Driving." His voice showed his impatience.

"Driving? Why on earth would I want to go driving first thing in the morning? Besides, I already know how to drive." It was difficult for him not to smile.

Luke sat down on the chair between the two. He was used to his father's teasing and was learning to outsmart him.

"Sure. Let's go," James said as he laid the book down and rose from his seat.

"Good-bye, boys. Please be careful," Beth said as her two boys started to leave.

"We will," said Luke.

"Say a prayer for me," James whispered in her ear.

"Oh, James, it can't be that bad to teach Luke to drive."

James kissed Beth on the cheek and followed Luke.

Luke jumped into the driver's seat, anxious to take his first lesson. He started the car and pushed the clutch in with his left foot and grabbed for the gear shift, per his father's instructions.

Screech, the gears complained as he forced the car into reverse.

James could feel his nerves stand on end. He tried to remind himself this was only Luke's first attempt and to be patient.

Luke backed up slowly and to his left. He then attempted to put the engine into first as the gears ground on each other loudly. "Sorry."

"Are you talking to me or the poor gears you just mated unwillingly?"

"Father," Luke said with a hint of embarrassment.

"Yes, Luke?"

"You can't mate gears."

"Didn't you just leave part of one with the other," he said, teasing the blushing boy.

"Father," he said again, "I won't do it again."

"Good," he said with a slight smile on his face.

The car pulled forward in a jerking motion.

"Luke, you must let the clutch out slowly."

"Stop," said James as he glanced towards the house.

Luke slammed his foot on the brake pedal, forcing the occupants forward rapidly.

"What's wrong?" he asked in a panic.

"There's your mother. She wants us." He pointed toward the house where she stood near the front gate, waving her hand in the air.

"Pull over there and roll down the window to see what she wants."

"James, the hospital called. They need you. Mrs. Foley is in labor with the twins."

"Well, Luke, I guess we'll have to continue the driving lessons later."

"Okay, just let me park it," Luke said in one last effort to drive just a little further. He pulled forward slightly and turned a little too hard and rode up on the curb.

"Stop, Luke, or you'll be on top of the fence, soon," James said excitedly. His stomach tightened as he held tightly to the dashboard with his left hand and the back of the seat with his right.

"Darn! I wish you weren't the town doctor," said Luke in a disgusted and angry tone of voice.

"Luke, I'm needed," he said in an effort to make him understand.

"I need you too," he said as he got out. He slammed the door.

"Luke, you must try to understand."

"Well, I don't," he yelled as he turned to go.

James knew he would have to deal with Luke's anger later. He loved his son dearly but wanted Luke to understand his love for the people who needed and depended on him.

His thoughts quickly turned to Mrs. Foley as he hurried to the hospital to deliver the twins.

CHAPTER SEVENTEEN

1953

She heard his footsteps bounce up the wooden steps and the screen door swing open. She laid the dish towel on the beige tiled sink and hurried to welcome him.

"Hello, dear. How was your day?" She reached for his white jacket as he removed it.

"Guess what?" he said in his usual jovial manner.

"How many clues do I get?"

"Someone is coming to visit from far away."

She could tell it was someone he liked by the smile on his face and the twinkle in his eyes. "Let's see who it could be," she said as he kissed her hello. "It's Henry," she said, sure she was right since he always kept in touch with him.

"No."

"No? Who then?" She was puzzled. They didn't have many visitors in the small town in which they lived, but when they did it had always been old friends. Her mind was blank.

"Charles," he said triumphantly as if he had won the game.

"Are you teasing, James? What on earth is he doing coming way out here? He never goes anywhere. Is he bringing the family? When will he arrive? How long will they stay?"

"Hold on. I'll explain it all if you promise to feed me dinner first." He could smell the fresh baked bread. His nose seemed to lead his body in the direction of the kitchen.

"Okay," she said impatiently as she followed him.

He sat down while she busied herself preparing the meal for the table.

"They'll be here Saturday afternoon."

"This Saturday. Two days from now?" she interrupted.

"Yes, dear. Now, if I may finish," he said teasingly.

"Oh, sorry. Please do go on."

"He's bringing three of the four children. Marcy, the oldest, is away at school like Luke. Charles claims he just came home one day last week and decided it was time to go visit old friends before the old friends weren't around to visit anymore." He began to dish up the stew she had placed in front of him. He made a special effort to scoop up several of the large orange carrots from the thick gravy. The white mushy dumplings bounced about as he searched the stew for his favorites. The hot steaming air rose against his hand as he stirred.

"Is Catherine coming, too?" she asked anxiously.

"Yes. I don't suppose he would attempt the trip alone with three children and no warden, do you?"

Charles had later returned to medical school and had become a well-known and well-respected internist since he found that business was not his forte. He had also become well-known for child spoiling. His children would have been absolute monsters on the loose if it hadn't been for his wife, who had to take an extra hard role with the children to compensate for Charles's extreme leniency.

"No, I'm not sure anyone could manage it without Catherine along to keep them in line." She smiled at him as she began to dish up her own meal. "Remember when they visited several years ago?" she reminded James. "I dare say the children left a definite, not altogether favorable, impression on any human brave enough to get near them. Remember the smallest one. What was his name?"

"Josh, I think," James contributed.

"He laid that awful smelly dead mouse he found under the porch, in my lap." She laughed out loud. "I don't think I've ever be so startled. Catherine thought I was going to jump right in her lap."

He laughed with her. "He was a little dickens. He probably still is," he added. "The stew is great. Sweetheart."

"Thank you. How long will they stay?" Her apprehension was clear, now that she spoke of the children's personalities.

"Only two days."

She let out a sigh of relief. "I guess I can manage for two days. I do hope there are no dead mice nearby, though."

"Don't worry, dear. Charles is an extremely successful doctor and cannot possibly change his plans in order to extend his stay."

"*That's reassuring.*"

"*I can hardly wait to tell Charles about the lab and show him all of our suspended-animation equipment. The new capsule will be here tomorrow. I couldn't have timed it better if I had tried.*" His excitement rose as did his voice at the thought of sharing his secret world with his old friend.

"*Do you think he'll understand your enthusiasm for immortality?*" she said as she passed him the dark green bread basket. "*More bread, dear?*"

"*Yes, thank you.*"

The soft white bread was still warm to the touch. He held it in his hand as he stared into space for a moment. "*Understand? Maybe not.*" The butter melted quickly on the warm bread. "*But I think he'll become just as excited as I when he realizes this new scientific adventure actually exists and is in the very near stages of being utilized as a means of prolonging life.*

He ate the bread in only a few bites. He was so easily worked up about this new frontier, and his excitement burst forth whenever he started talking about it.

"*James, dear,*" she paused before continuing, "*you must be cautious with people who have never encountered your new frontier.*"

He looked at her and listened intently.

"*Not everyone has the love of life you do, dear, and very few people feel the boundless rejection of death that you do.*"

There was a long silence. He laid his fork down and leaned back in his chair. "*You're right, Beth,*" he said quietly. "*You're right. I will do my best to act prudently.*"

He pushed his plate away. His heart ached at the memory of his dear mother. Yes, he thought, I do totally reject death.

He that hath ears to hear,
let him hear.

Luke 14:35

CHAPTER EIGHTEEN

Jason had given Kelly his reassuring smile when he entered the recovery room. He worried that his anxiety might give her a clue for the chaotic ticking of his mind as he lovingly watched his son sleeping.

Everything had always seemed to be black and white to Jason. The answers were always evident if one cared to see them, and now his son's existence began to become a horror story. Maybe he had always accepted the easiest answers and now this slap-in-the-face incident had awakened him. There was definitely more to this occurrence than met the eye. Damn, what on earth went on in that operating room, he thought. He pictured a little defenseless body of a child, his child, on the operating table with doctors and nurses crowding over him, pushing and shoving for a small amount of space to view the phenomenon. The other part of Jason's mind tried to gain control as it always had, but he was having great difficulty. The fighting side of his mind burst in with, that's ridiculous, as it continued to give off visions of little Danny clumsily crawling away, giggling loudly as his Daddy chased him on hands and knees. Come on, Jason. Grab hold of yourself, he thought. Surely Kelly will see the concern on your face. He needed to put it out of his mind for now. It would accomplish nothing at this time and place.

He slowly put it out of his mind as he stared at his little man lying there with his head wrapped neatly in snow white bandages. His eyes showed movement. A sign he would wake up soon.

"Nurse, he's waking up, I think," Kelly said.

A dark-haired, dark-eyed nurse, who had just come on duty, looked up from her paperwork at the desk. She rose and walked towards the bed.

"Yes, it looks as if he is. We'll strap his hands down for a while to prevent any reactive movement towards his head. Just until he's fully awake." She did so and proceeded to check his vital signs, and notated the chart next to the bed. "Everything is fine. He'll sleep a great deal for the next day or two. That was a big operation for such a small fellow." She went back to the main desk in the middle of the intensive care unit and left Jason and Kelly in their silent vigil.

Danny's big brown eyes opened slowly but as wide as always. He still looked very sleepy.

"Good afternoon, sweetheart." Kelly gently ran her fingers on his cheek. He turned his head slightly to make sure his Daddy was there also.

"Hello, little man." Danny smiled as Jason spoke, then closed his eyes and seemed to go back to sleep.

The nurses had been watching from the desk. She approached the bed once again.

"He'll sleep most of the day, off and on. He knows you're with him now. Maybe you should go relax a bit and come back later. We'll take extra special care of him for you."

Jason watched the nurse as she cared for his boy. She smiled at Kelly, and Kelly returned the smile. Jason could sense the camaraderie between the two. She must have children of her own, he thought. Kelly then smiled at Jason when she notice him watching her. He could tell she felt better now that Danny was out of surgery even if he hadn't quite woke up yet.

"Thanks," he said to the nurse. "Maybe that would be best for now." He took Kelly's hand and they turned to leave.

They had been in and out of the intensive care room all day and had become worn out mentally as well as physically.

Kelly slept restfully in the large comfortable bed. Jason sat on the love seat and watched her as his mind began racing again, preoccupied with the strange occurrence of this morning's operation. He felt insecure and scared. He needed the love and security he had so often given to Kelly and the people around him. He needed someone to put their arms around him, hold him tight, and tell him it would be all right, as he had done so many times for others. He felt a chill as he sat there on the velvet love seat with the large picturesque window behind him. He watched as the city's lights turned on a few at a time, breaking the darkness of the night. The scene before him reminded him of when he was a child camping with his family. The fireflies darting from here to there through the darkness, on a mission known only to them, in the night's still air. His thoughts faded as his need for warmth overcame his need for tranquility.

He quietly eased into bed so as not to wake Kelly. He wanted to be next to her warm body without waking her. He nudged over and watched her breathe peacefully. She was his sleeping beauty just like in the story books. He stroked her fine strawberry-blond hair. The soft curls felt like satin to his fingertips. His urge to be held and loved grew. He leaned towards her and kissed her forehead with a long, loving kiss that was as gentle as the morning dew resting on the new rose petals opening to welcome the sunrise. His longing for love grew stronger, and was no longer only an urge. It was now a very demanding need crying out to be fulfilled. He began kissing her sleepy lips, and his hands ran over the baby-soft skin of her breasts which lay peacefully exposed below the covers.

She began to wake in a dreamlike, uninhabited state. The gentle kisses and soft touch of skin to skin seemed more intense than in a waking state. The city lights in the far-off background added a shadow of tenderness. She kissed Jason in return, put her arms around his neck and held him tight as she became more awake with each minute that passed.

"I love you, Kelly. I need you. Never, never leave me, my darling," he whispered.

She could sense his need for her. She felt his intense love pouring out from every inch of his being. She returned the love willingly and with pleasure, never even concerned with the fact that she had not taken any precautionary measures against pregnancy. The warmth of the Jason's body next to hers increased the passion she felt for him. Jason kissed her all over her body and his hands touched every inch of her, caressing her gently and lovingly. He did not hurry to enter her, but was slow and passionate. He prolonged her pleasure with his touch and then entered her slowly. His body moved rhythmically, slowly in and out until they came together in a climax that made her feel like one with Jason.

It had been many years since either of them had felt the carefree flow of love and passion.

Kelly had faithfully taken one form or another of birth control since learning of Danny's deformity. She had no desire to bring another child into the world unless and until her firstborn's condition could be remedied. However, the persistent fear of creating another abnormal child had not been present this time as it had each time they had made love in the past.

They both fell asleep with the contentedness only love could bring to the heart and to the body.

CHAPTER NINETEEN

1965

Luke was finally going to come home. He had been gone for so very long, thought James, as he sat on the porch swing waiting for Beth to finish dressing so they could be on their way to the train depot.

"Come on, Beth. I don't want to be late," he said in a raised voice.

She didn't answer. He knew she would hurry, but they were both so very eager to get their first look at their new grandson, Michael.

As he sat waiting, he thought about how amazing it was that Luke and his bride of six years would chose to move back home. He guessed the big city had lost its allure. Even though Luke had achieved a successful career in a large accounting firm, it was difficult or impossible to remove the small town upbringing from a boy of any age.

The new baby was only a few months old. The long trip would be hard on the little fellow, but James could not wait to get his arms around the tiny, warm bundle. His own bloodline carried forward, he thought with satisfaction as he impatiently glanced down at his watch. He knew there was still plenty of time, but he felt antsy to get going.

"Beth, are you ready yet?" he yelled again. God, I wish we could have had more children, he thought as he again glanced down at his watch.

"Beth," he said again when he heard the squeak of the screen door as it opened.

"Yes, darling. I'm ready. I don't think I've ever seen you so impatient." She stepped outside and closed the door behind her. "We're leaving awfully early, aren't we?"

"Never too early. Never too early," he said as he got out of the swing. "This is my first chance to see my new grandson. He wouldn't appreciate my being late for our first meeting."

"No, I guess he wouldn't," she replied, as they headed for the car. "It's been such a long time since I've held a baby, I wonder if I remember how."

"Of course you do. You're a natural-born mother. Or should I say grandmother, now?"

"Oh James, that sounds so very old." She grimaced.

"I'm so pleased Luke finally decided to come home where he belongs."

"James, Luke had to prove himself as an accountant in the big city first. You're not being fair," she said as if she were scolding a child.

"He's been away too many years," he said scornfully.

"I'm not leaving this house with you until I hear a change of attitude in your voice. The last thing Luke needs on his first day home is a lecture." She paused and waited for his response, but he was silent. "Luke would never have had an opportunity to cultivate his large clients without spending those years in the city."

"Yes, Beth. I am well aware of that, but he's my only child. I've been unable to watch him mature and share the last six years with him." He was silent for a while as they got into the car and headed for town.

"Do you remember the time you attempted to teach Luke to drive and instead you had to rush over to the hospital to deliver babies?"

"Yes."

"Well, Luke had to do something very important away from us. You tried so hard to make him understand your position and the responsibilities you assumed in your life. Now it's your turn to understand him and what responsibilities he took on in his life." She paused briefly. "I know you treasure Luke, dear, but it's unfair to put a burden upon him simply because he's an only child."

The silence that filled the air bothered him. It felt like a wall between them.

After fifteen minutes of silence, she began again. "It would have been wonderful to have had more children, but we couldn't. Now we should be thankful for a new grandson and—"

"By God, you're right, Beth," he said matter-of-factly. "I really wasn't looking at that side of it."

"And don't forget we have a daughter-in-law whom we hardly know. We'll have to make sure Mary feels welcome to our family, too."

"Okay, Beth, okay. I'm sold. From this moment on, we do have new people to treasure, and we will make Luke's bride feel like family." His voice changed to sound less disgruntled and he began to smile.

97

"Good," Beth said with a sigh of relief.

She was glad to hear him put his anger behind him after so much time and take on a new attitude. It had bothered her for some time now that James was so upset that Luke had chosen to live far from home. Today was the day all of that nonsense could be put behind them, and she was pleased to see James do so.

After several minutes had passed, James said joyfully, "you know, Beth, my father would have been awfully proud to know his great-grandson had been named after him."

"Yes, I'm sure he would have."

They were approaching the train station as James remembered how Luke had always favored the train to any other form of transportation. Even as a little boy, he had loved trains. Maybe all little boys did, he thought as he chose a prime parking space. He knew what his first present for his grandson would be. He paced the platform while checking his watch every few minutes. He noticed that Beth sat patiently watching him. He wondered what she was thinking as she smiled at him walking up and down, watching for the train to approach. He rubbed his hands together as if scratching the palm of one with the palm of the other.

Beth looked quizzically at him. "Are you cold, James?"

"No. Just warming my hands so that when I hold Michael they won't be cold for him."

She laughed.

"Here it comes," he said as he stood erect with tension.

Beth stood up and walked next to him. She put her gloved hand through his arm and held on. He patted her hand.

"Here he comes," he said excitedly as he turned and kissed her check.

"You're like a little boy waiting to open your birthday presents." She smiled at him with love. "I guess we never really grow up. I feel blessed to have a husband that loves his family so very much."

He turned to her. "I'm so glad you know how much I love you and our family."

Then he turned back as the train came to a slow stop in front of them. The odor of dirt and oil rushed past as the train moved by. Luke was waiting to jump off the moment it came to a halt with his wife and newborn son behind him. He helped his wife down the steps and hurried to his parents with his arms open wide.

"Mother. Father." He hugged them both. They then hugged Luke's pretty wife.

"Welcome home Mary," said James. "May I?" he asked as he held his arms out in a cradled position.

"Certainly." She handed him the tiny bundle.

He carefully pulled the blanket back to peer inside. Soft gray-blue eyes stared up at the stranger as the small fair-skinned hands clasped onto one another. He carefully touched the soft tender skin of the baby's cheek and could smell the fresh, clean aroma babies always seem to have. The eyes of innocence and wonder looked up at him as he watched the babies every move.

"He's beautiful. Look Beth," he said as he leaned toward his wife without offering the small bundle to her.

"He's precious." She lowered the blanket enough to see his full face. She didn't attempt to hold the baby. It was clear that James was not going to give up the baby any time soon.

Luke and his wife had not yet found a home and would be staying with his parents for a while. This would give James and Beth time to become acquainted with the new family members.

Love possesses not, nor would it be possessed,
for love is sufficient unto love.

K. Gibran

CHAPTER TWENTY

The next day was much better than the day before. Danny was awake more of the time and was doing very well considering what he had been though. Kelly felt very strong, brave and secure with the hopefulness of Danny's recovery and Jason's total love and need for her. It had always been her who needed him, but now she felt he too needed her.

The days began to pass quickly. Danny's words were becoming much clearer than they had been but still not up to his age level. The doctor's prognosis was very good and Danny was doing better than they had expected.

Jason and Kelly had had the time to discover the surroundings of the new city. It had been a long time since Kelly could remember the delight of simply listening to the musical sounds of a bird chirping in the trees above. It had felt as if someone had removed an extremely heavy burden from her shoulders, if only for a while. It felt fantastic. She knew Danny was being well cared for at the hospital, and hope grew each day as he recovered from the surgery. If it wouldn't have looked as though she had recently escaped from an asylum, she would have skipped down the street singing, she thought. She thanked God above for everything in sight and for the most important person she could ever know and who was also her best friend, Jason.

It would only be a couple of days more and they would take Danny home, which pleased her. For now, she would flit around feeling happiness and love, much like a butterfly from flower to flower.

CHAPTER TWENTY-ONE

1967

The day had been full, and it seemed longer than previous days at the hospital and lab. James hurried home with a large square package wrapped in bright red paper under his arm. His steps were faster than normal as his anticipation of Michael's excitement regarding the package grew.

Michael would be two years old today, and the party was to be held at Gramma's and Grampa's house.

He bounced up the steps with his white jacket flapping open at the bottom, front edges. He flung the screen door open. It squeaked out its familiar welcome as James entered.

"I'm home," he yelled as he set down the package and headed for the kitchen where all the delicious smells seemed to be coming from.

Michael hurried to meet him. It seemed as though his feet couldn't catch up with his body which leaned forward far ahead of the little feet.

"Papa," he cried with excitement. "Papa."

"Hello, Michael," he said, as he scooped his blond grandson up into his arms. "So you're two years old today, are you?"

Michael nodded in agreement. He then spotted the bright red surprise. He looked straight into his grandfather's eyes and asked, "Mike's?"

"I'm not sure," he teased. "Is Michael the little boy with a birthday today?"

"Uh-huh," he said, as he watched his grandfather's smiling eyes.

"Go ahead. You can open it." James set the package on the floor as

Michael quickly wiggled out of the large powerful arms and hurried toward the package sitting on the floor.

"No, no," he heard behind him James and Michael turned at the same time to see Michael's mommy standing at the kitchen door, wiping her hands with the yellow calico apron wrapped about her.

Michael then looked up at his grandpa with pleading eyes.

"Ah come on, just this one," James said as he turned his own pleading eyes toward Michael's mother. "I've already said he could."

She surveyed the eyes of both boys, large and small, and slowly replied, "okay, but just this one."

Beth came to the doorway and stood behind Mary to watch the excitement. Michael began to rip the paper wildly.

"Train," he said loudly.

James knelt down to help him retrieve it from the hard cardboard box. "It's a caboose," he told Michael. "A red caboose for your train set."

Michael squealed with delight and did his best to hold onto the one foot tall by two foot wide, bright red caboose.

"It's beautiful, said Beth, as she approached to kiss James hello, after which she bent over to pick up the torn wrapping paper scattered about the floor.

"Come on, Michael. Let's go outside and try it out," he said as he looked at the two women for approval.

"That's fine," said Beth. "Luke should be here shortly. We'll call you when dinner is ready."

"Great." He grabbed Michael in one arm, the caboose in the other, and headed for the door. As he started down the steps, Luke was just arriving.

"Hello, son," said James. "Come on out back with us. We're going to try out our new toy."

James and Luke had set up a miniature electric train, big enough for Michael to ride, under the patio out back. The wisteria trailed across the top of the patio cover with soft purple and white grape-like clusters of petals which filled the air with a soft sweet fragrant smell.

"What's that you've got there?" Luke asked his father.

"A caboose, of course. What good is a train without a red caboose?"

Luke followed them to the train set. James hooked the caboose onto the existing engine and passenger car.

"All aboard," he yelled and then proceeded to help Michael into the passenger car. Luke sat on the wooden patio chair behind the two.

"Hey, that's a great caboose, Michael," Luke said, as he watched his son's excitement.

"Papa. Papa," Michael said.

"Papa's pretty nice for getting you such a nice present, isn't he?"

Michael nodded in agreement as he anxiously sat, waiting for the train to move.

James started the train and allowed it to slowly move around the track. He turned to Luke but remained near the train set in case Michael decided to get off before his grandfather could turn it off. "How was your day, son?"

"Hectic as ever, Dad. That's really a nice caboose. It must have cost you a few bucks."

"It's only money and Michaels worth it. He sure likes trains. I guess he gets that from you."

"Yeah." Luke said and laughed.

They sat watching Michael circle the track several times.

"You're a good grandfather, Dad," Luke said.

"Thank you, Son."

"And a good father, too."

"Well, thank you Luke. I appreciate that," he smiled with pride.

"I hope someday I can be like you," Luke said as he watched his son circle. "The whole town loves you, you know."

"Oh, now stop it, Luke. I can feel my head swelling."

"You know, Dad, when I was young I never realized how much you gave to this town. Now that I've been back here for a while, I realize how important giving life and preserving life is to you and how much you've given of yourself to others."

James turned to look at Luke. "Who have you been talking to?"

"Some of the older residents in town. They think the world of you."

"Well, that's quite a compliment but not near as nice as my own son telling me I'm a good father and grandfather. My family means everything to me. Always has."

"It shows, Dad. I hope one day Michael will feel the same about me."

"He will, son, he will."

"James, Luke, Michael, dinner's ready," a female voice called.

When there is no vision,
the people will perish.

Solomon, Book of Proverbs 29:18

Chapter Twenty-Two

The day had come. Today Danny would return home. His recovery had gone better than expected. His motor responses were improving to a moderate extent and were predicted to get progressively better as time went on. All the postoperative X-rays looked good. The small bit of tumor that could not be reached appeared to be a dormant piece of matter lying within the brain.

Danny was dressed, and Kelly was putting his small knit cap on his head over his partially grown hair. Jason walked into the room in his usual jovial manner.

"What a beautiful blue cap you have, young man," he said as he held his arms wide for Danny.

"Daddy," Danny yelled with excitement and held his arms out for his father. Danny held a special affection for his father, and it was always evident the moment Jason entered his surroundings.

"Everything is taken care of. There's a taxi waiting outside, and a volunteer will be up for the bags," said Jason as he grabbed his son.

Kelly kissed her two men as they intertwined in a three-way hug.

"Are you ready to go in the big airplane, little man? Gramma and Grampa will be waiting to see you." Jason turned toward Kelly, "I talked to your parents. They said they'd be at the airport early, to flag the plane in." He laughed as Danny clapped his best to show his delight.

The taxi maneuvered brilliantly through the morning post-rush-hour traffic to the airport.

Once aboard the airplane, the flight seemed much longer than it had coming to Dallas. Danny slept, more out of boredom than anything else.

It would be good to see her parents and to sleep in her own bed. Kelly was grateful for the parents she had been given. They were there like a genie out of a bottle, whenever Kelly seemed to need them, and they always knew exactly when that was. Kelly had to do incredibly little asking of favors, since they offered before she could ask. Kelly reflected on Jason's philosophy. Maybe there was a reason for everything and everyone who surrounded them, she thought.

The pilot announced their position, weather, and time of arrival. It would only be thirty minutes before they landed.

Kelly was unaware of it at the time, but the emotional weight that had been lifted from her at the hospital was again beginning to rest upon her shoulders.

She closed her eyes and laid her head back as the captain finished speaking. She gave her little sleeping prince a squeeze as she silently asked the Lord to continue to give her strength and to release Danny from his physical confinement. Then she dozed off for a short time.

"Honey, we're landing," she heard Jason say as he nudged her arm.

"It will feel great to be back at work and have things back to normal," Jason said.

"It sure will," replied Kelly.

Danny also woke up. They were the first people off the plane.

"Look, Danny, there's Gramma and Grampa." He waved in their direction. Hugs abounded just inside the flight gates.

"How's our little man?" said Gramma as she took Danny into her arms and kissed him many times.

"Let's take care of the luggage, Dad." Jason put his arm around the shoulders of Kelly's father. "We'll tell you all about it on the way home."

Kelly was pleased Jason had long ago accepted Kelly's parents as his own, since his had been deceased for some time.

It took half an hour to gather up the luggage. It didn't seem to matter how far or how fast technology progressed, the airports would most likely never find a quick and easy way to rescue one's luggage, thought Kelly, as they stood waiting.

On the ride home Kelly and Jason talked incessantly, sometimes simultaneously. Danny was enthralled with all the excitement and gaiety.

The fact that the doctors couldn't get all of the tumor pleased no one, but then no one could deny that Danny's motor responses where obviously improving.

"Do the doctors expect complete or partial normalcy from this operation?" asked Grampa, who was usually an extremely quiet and reserved person and somewhat pessimistic.

"If the improvement of motor responses keeps progressing at the rate they are now going, Dr. Hess sees no reason Daniel Robert Ashley cannot be as normal as you or I." Jason laughed. "That is, if we're normal." He beamed with pride that Danny was doing so well.

Everyone laughed and Danny clapped his hands with joy.

The trip had been a long one, and as they pulled into the driveway of their home, Jason sighed. "Home sweet Home."

CHAPTER TWENTY-THREE

1968

James knocked on the solid wood door and while waiting for someone to answer he looked down at the multi-colored paint splotches which sporadically covered his green work pants. He was picking at a large pale blue glob with his fingernail located just above his left knee when he heard the latch turn and saw the door opening.

"Good morning, Dad," a sleepy voice said.

"Good morning, Luke. Are you ready to get to work?"

"As ready as I'll ever be," Luke said quietly. "Painting has never been my favorite pastime."

James entered and put his arm around Luke. "It's all in the attitude, son."

Drawn by the rich smell of strong coffee, they headed toward the kitchen.

"Dad, come have a cup of coffee before we start." He yawned and let out a sort of growl.

"Not quite awake yet, Luke?" James could tell Luke would rather be in bed on this beautiful Saturday morning. "You'll feel better once you get out in the fresh air. It's really a gorgeous morning." The cool air had thoroughly awakened and refreshed James during the walk to Luke's new but old fixer-upper home. "Do you have any orange juice?" he asked.

"Sure, Doc." Luke opened the refrigerator door and searched through the various bottles that sat on the top shelf. "I guess it is the healthier choice," he said as he twisted off the top and poured it into a glass.

James was careful to take good care of his body. He intended it to last him a long time. "Michael still asleep?"

"Well, he is for now, but he's an early riser. He'll be up soon. I'm ready to start, if you are. I'll go get some work clothes on." Luke put his coffee cup on the sink and headed upstairs.

"Okay, let's get to it," James said and set his glass near Luke's cup.

Luke had readied all the brushes, ladders, and paint equipment the night before on the long, narrow porch. This was the farthest area from the bedrooms, which were in the rear of the house, so the two men would not wake Luke's sleeping pregnant wife and Michael.

James knew they would get more accomplished before Michael woke, but missed his pesky presence anyway.

The sun was new to the day, and its light was still soft and gentle on its recipients.

James pried at the top of the metal can with a flathead screwdriver. He lifted it off, releasing the fumes of the oil-based, exterior paint. The paint dripped onto his fingers before he could put the top on the newspapers below the can.

"Pretty color," James said, as he added the fresh paint to the myriad of old crusty paint on his pants.

"Pink seems to be the in color," Luke replied as he set up his ladder against the house.

James handed Luke a small amount of paint he had poured into an empty coffee can. The paint ran down one side. It was obvious they were not the neatest of house painters.

"I'll work the top of the porch, Dad, if you'll work the bottom."

"Sure. If you drip paint guess who gets it?" He laughed. He began his work while humming to himself. James had always enjoyed rising with the sun. It made him feel refreshed and as newborn as the day itself. Luke, on the other hand, had always been a sleeper. James could remember the mornings he would have to prod Luke into getting out of bed. He swore the boy could sleep for fourteen hours every night.

The sun's rays grew brighter as the day moved on, and it warmed the senses as it seemed to stretch and spread its energy across the earth.

"How's Mary feeling, Luke?" he said, breaking the concentrated silence.

"She experiences morning sickness every morning, but other than that, she's doing fine."

"That'll probably stop soon, usually after the first three months." He returned to the larger can of paint to refill his smaller can with paint.

"It did last time, I think . . . Doc."

James was aware of Luke's chide. He was not the obstetrician for Luke's wife. They had chosen a big-city doctor. This was not offensive to James since he was working primarily with the cryogenic suspension now. He had grown used to everyone in town calling him Doc, everyone except his family.

He knelt down among the lilies just behind the porch. As he did, they seemed to release a sweet-and-sour smell as he rustled them in an effort to reach the bottom of the house.

Luke had also finished with the porch and was moving his ladder to the same side of the house his father was on.

"I think I hear movement inside," Luke said.

"Well, it's about time they got up. Let's get Michael out here to help," he said teasingly.

"Help? I'm afraid it would be anything but help, Dad."

"How's the boy supposed to learn, Luke?"

"Dad, don't put any ideas into his head or there'll be paint everywhere, except on the house.

"He's an active little fellow, isn't he?"

"Very active." Luke climbed up the ladder above his father.

"Does that mean you're hoping for a girl this time?"

"Heck, I'm not particular. Besides, Mary wants a big family, so I'm sure we'll get a girl in there somewhere. Six, maybe."

"Six, maybe? I hope you like working, son."

"Sure, Dad, just like you." He laughed. "Remember the time I got so upset because I wanted to learn to drive and you had to rush off to the hospital and deliver someone's twins?"

"Yeah, Mrs. Foley's. Now there's a big family. She finally stopped after fourteen children."

"Well, that may be her opinion of big, but it's not mine. Six will do just fine."

"Count your blessing, son. You're lucky to be able to have them. There's nothing more important than family," he said solemnly. He then heard the door open and leaned over towards the porch. A small figure approached wearing stripped pajamas a few sizes too big.

"Good morning, Michael," said James.

"Morning,' the sleepy little boy said. The hair in the back of his head stood on end.

"Are you going to come help Grampa?"

He nodded and turned around toward the door.

A few minutes later a much more rambunctious boy came through the front door and down the steps.

"No, Michael," his father said as Michael attempted to pick up a brush dripping with paint that sat on top of his grandfather's paint can.

"Come on, Michael," his Grampa said as he took his hand. He led him back to the porch and allowed him to pick out an unused brush from the painting equipment. "You can pretend to paint with us." He then went back to his work, followed by the little shadow.

Michael stood about and watched attentively for hours, pretending to paint everything in sight.

Luke was already on the other side of the house, still painting the uppermost portion of the house while James painted as far as he could reach without a ladder.

"Dad," Luke called.

James stopped his own work, laid down his brush, and went to the side of the house Luke was on.

"Can you help me with this ladder so I can reach the second level?"

"Sure. I'll hold it. You go ahead." James held tight as Luke climbed down the unsteady ladder, carrying his paint can.

"Thanks, Dad. I'll yell when I need you again."

James headed back to his work area but stopped short. He watched as long as he could before he burst out laughing. Michael had picked up his Grampa's brush, dipped it, handle and all, into the paint and had begun to help the two older men paint the house. Michael had pink paint dripping down his hand and onto his arm. The front of him was covered in pink, as well.

Michael turned toward his grampa, froze, and began to cry. James knew he sensed trouble in the air, probably a spanking.

"What's going on?" yelled Luke from the ladder.

"Your son is helping us out," James called back.

Luke could not get near enough to the edge to see, so James took Michael's hand and led the tearful boy farther from the house for his father to see. Luke began to laugh, too.

Mary ran out to the porch to see what all the commotion was about. "Oh no!" she said, as she put her hand to her mouth in amazement.

"It's okay, Michael. Don't cry," his grandfather reassured him.

He looked up at his grampa with a stunned look on his face as if to question that assertion.

"It's okay," he repeated as he knelt down next to Michael, and wiped his tears with his fingertips. He looked up at Mary. "Sorry, Mary. I shouldn't have left the brush where he could reach it."

"It's all right, Dad," she said as she headed down the stairs and began to see the humor.

"Do you have a camera and film handy?" James asked her.

"Yes, I think so. I'll go see." She turned on the steps and went back inside.

"Luke, come on down. Let's take a picture of our helper." He called up, as he went to hold the ladder.

Michael stood still, frozen with amazement.

Mary returned with the camera and took several photos of the painters, tall and small.

She then took the apprentice painter inside to change him. "I'll keep this worker inside for a while," she said as Luke and his father resumed their work.

Faith is the substance of things hoped for,
The evidence of things not seen.

Hebrews 11:1

CHAPTER TWENTY-FOUR

The hospital had been hectic, and Dr. Hess was looking forward to his few days off before returning to his home in San Francisco. He had chosen never to marry. His family and life were the hospital and its staff, and his children were the ones who came to him in great need. He knew he could never neglect a wife or child the way so many surgeons did. He knew they did so out of love and devotion for their occupation, but this was his only purpose for life.

Although he hungered for home, it was not as close as he wished it were. He would catch a flight for Connecticut this evening and would speak with Dr. Connectivich tomorrow, as arranged. It had taken several letters and many weeks before he had received a reply from Dr. Connectivich, and he was overly anxious to meet and speak with this gentleman with the novel name and the genius mind.

The flight was rough, and the food was cold. To make the trip complete, Dr. Hess had spilled his bourbon and seven in his lap when the plane hit a strong wind current, making it appear as though he had wet his pants.

The plane landed in the large airport of Litchfield, Connecticut, population 4,568. The rented car would be waiting. Thank goodness for secretaries who handled all the arrangements ahead of time, and his was exceptional at travel arrangements. He decided to wait until he reached his destination to change clothes, since he was not a man who embarrassed easily. The little town was almost one hundred miles away from the airport, and by the time he arrived at the bed and breakfast, he would welcome a shower and some rest.

The car agency supplied the map he would need for his trip. He traveled lightly, taking only one carry-on suitcase, in order to avoid the usual baggage retrieval complications.

The drive was pleasant. The surrounding land was green with new growth. Large old trees lined many of the roads, which usually led to small, older towns of minute populations. Nearly two hours had passed, and his stomach began to growl for nourishment. The stain had dried into a noticeable spot on his light brown slacks. Hopefully, the bed and breakfast owner would be able to launder the slacks, since he had only one other pair with him.

The weather-beaten, barely legible sign at the side of the road told him he had arrived in Darda, population 225. He drove on. The large, tall trees shaded the roadway, and small farmhouses dotted the scenery. Some were abandoned and in disrepair; others simply old.

Two twenty-five. If he added the digits together, they totaled nine. That was the number of love, compassion, patience, universality, tolerance, and endings. He laughed to himself, as well as at himself. Once analytical, always analytical, he thought. He searched his mind as he tried to remember who had gotten him interested in numerology. His thoughts conjured up Nancy's blue eyes peering over her surgical mask. It was she who had been so involved and gotten his interest by using his name and birth place as an example.

He then remembered that one of his Hebrew college friends had named his first daughter Darda, explaining it meant pearl of wisdom or some such thing. It had been a long drive. His mind was wandering down strange paths.

The main street was near. It was narrow. As he approached the inhabitants watched the unfamiliar car drive up, well aware it was a stranger, but continuing on about their business after a first glance. The stores and buildings were well kept, but the construction design made the period of architecture unmistakable. If he removed the asphalt paving on the street and inserted a horse and buggy, all would fit very picturesquely.

The bed and breakfast establishment was easy to find. It was one of the larger buildings on the street, with a balcony on the second floor that ran the length of the structure. The lace curtains of old lined the windows, and the front door had beveled, frosted glass. Most of the buildings were of the original wood color with a walkway made of planks in front of them. He parked on the side of the building, since it was the only apparent place for a vehicle. It would feel good to rest a while. It was late afternoon, and he did not need to be anywhere until evening.

He entered and immediately felt comfortable in the vintage setting. He stopped to survey the room and the romance it radiated. There was an antique aroma to the room, almost musty, but not quite. In the center of the room was the circular couch of deep maroon velvet with buttons tucked deep into the material every four or five inches, making a beautiful pattern. The velvet showed very little wear, and the orange-red fringe at the bottom hung to touch the floor. The hall tree to his left was of dark mahogany with brass hooks and a large oval mirror in the center. The grandfather clock, also of dark wood, chimed once, noting the half hour. Ahead of him was the desk, and to its right, a large staircase leading up to the second landing. He heard rustling and noticed someone coming from a back room. He approached the desk.

"Good afternoon. May I be of help?" said a rather heavyset, middle-aged women with deep red hair, obviously dyed. Her fragrance was strong, but pleasing, he thought.

"I'm Dr. Hess. I believe I have a reservation."

"You must be Doc's friend, ain't you? How do you do? My name is Bell. Anything I can help you with is my pleasure." She leaned her heavy frame towards the massive wooden desk, putting her weight on one arm. After she handed him the key, which had been on the front desk as if waiting for him, she rested the other arm on her large fleshy hip. "Room twelve will be yours. It's upstairs and has a view. That'll be six dollars a night, please. In advance." She paused and extended her hand. "Reasonable by any means, wouldn't you agree?"

"Yes, Bell, I would. Thank you," he said as he handed her ten dollars. "Keep it. Oh, by the way, I had a small mishap on the plane. He moved the sweater he was carrying in front of him to one side and looked down at the stain. "Could you tell me where I could have these slacks laundered?"

"I'll be happy to do it for ya, but don't be expecting nothing too fancy, will ya now?"

"Thanks, I'll bring them down later."

"What time would you like breakfast, sir?"

"I don't normally eat breakfast, Bell. Thanks anyway."

He proceeded up the steps, tired and ready to rest. He would eat later, he thought, as he lay down on the crocheted, beige bedspread without even a glance as to the remainder of the room. He fell to sleep quickly.

CHAPTER TWENTY-FIVE

1968

"So what are you going to shop for today, sweetheart?" James asked Beth, as she stood at the sink.

"Nothing special. I simply enjoy going to the city now and then," she said as she busied herself about the kitchen with the breakfast dishes. "I'll probably find something cute and cuddly for your next grandchild, though."

"When's the new baby due, anyway?" he asked as he brought his empty teacup to her.

"Any time now." She took the teacup. "Thanks."

He kissed her on the cheek and hugged her close with his right arm as he stood next to her.

"Those city doctors—." He stopped short. "Should Mary be riding the train with her time so close?"

"You're the doctor. Why ask me?" She twisted to look him squarely in the eye, waiting for an answer.

"Like I said, those city doctors." He left her side to search out his familiar white jacket. He seldom wore anything else, even in the coldest weather. He simply walked to work faster, building body heat.

"Well, I'll be going, Beth," he yelled from the front entry. He knew she would hurry to meet him for one more kiss at the door before he left.

"James, darling," as she hurried toward him. "Is there anything you'd like from the city while I'm there?"

"Well, if you happen to see a nice pipe, I could use a new one." He turned the knob with one hand and leaned to kiss her. "I'll miss you. Dress warmly and hurry home."

"I will. I love you, James."

They always expressed their love for each other verbally several times a day.

118

"I love you too, Beth. See you later." He shut the door behind him.

Beth busied herself getting ready. Luke, Mary and Michael would be there soon to pick her up. She went to the small mahogany table which held the telephone. She wrote, I'll love you forever, on the pad next to the phone. She heard the honk of a horn and hurried out the door and to the car.

James had made his morning rounds and was at his desk attending to paperwork. He had always preferred to get to work very early to get his pencil pushing out of the way before his morning rounds, but today he had chosen to spend what time he could with Beth since she would be so far away from their home in this small town. He stopped and looked up at the picture of Beth and Luke, long since outdated, on the corner of his large desk. He turned in his thickly padded, black leather chair to watch the gray squirrels scamper across the brown lawn as the patches of snow here and there melted under the transparent rays of the sun. The squirrels' thick winter coats rippled with movement as they ran from tree to tree across the stiff lawn, and their bushy, soft-looking tails stood on end as if filled with vitality. He watched one squirrel follow another up a tree. Varmints, just varmints, them gray-squirrels, he remembered an old farmer tell him once. It had been a quiet and peaceful morning, but he knew he had more important things to do today so he turned to finish his paperwork.

He glanced at his watch. It was 10:40 A.M. He rose from his desk and headed out the office door. His staff meeting was to begin at eleven.

Once all six staff doctors were seated, James started the meeting. "Good morning, gentlemen. Does anyone have any old business to discuss?"

Dr. Samson raised his hand and began to speak in his very deep voice. "What about the new equipment we discussed at the last meeting? It's badly needed."

"Yes, I'm aware of that, Dr. Samson. We've ordered it and expect it to arrive in four weeks," he said gently, knowing Dr. Samson had waited and pushed for a long time to acquire the needed equipment. Several times before it had become a heated subject, but at least this time it had been ordered.

There was a knock at the door, and a nurse entered. She spoke frantically, "Dr. Connectivich, we've been alerted that there's been a train accident. Two trains collided head-on. There are hundreds injured. It's only ten miles away, so a huge number of causalities will be brought here. The worst of them, I imagine."

"My God, could it be?" were his first softly spoken words as the other doctors watched him for direction. He turned his attention to them. He put his personal thoughts aside as he focused on the immediate needs of his staff. "Hurry, alert all personnel. Telephone everyone off duty and get them in here, stat." His family would have left hours ago, he thought, in an effort to reassure himself.

The doctors rushed out of the conference room with adrenaline pumping, preparing them for the avalanche of victims from the catastrophe which would be arriving soon.

James noticed the nurse standing in the doorway waiting for him to move into action. "Is there something wrong, Doctor?"

He lifted his eyes towards her. "Do you know which trains were involved in the collision?" Concern was scrawled across his face.

"No, I'm sorry, I don't. They just said two trains collided. But, the news said one was a passenger train, and the other a freight train. They said there's an enormous fire from the freight train which was carrying sulfur. Thank goodness, the wind isn't blowing in our direction. We'll probably get people coming in from breathing the sulfur air."

"Yes, no doubt we will. Thanks."

She shut the door behind her.

It couldn't be them, he thought. He tried desperately to dismiss the thought as he heard the first of many sirens, a sound that would last for hours. He tried again to put the thoughts of his family being on that train out of his mind. He hurried out of the room, knowing he would be needed, as well as everyone else available, to care for the injured.

Damn, I wish we had that new equipment now, he thought as he hurried to the emergency area to assist with triage.

The pace had slowed down after many hours of frenzied work. He could still smell the burned flesh of his patients, and he noticed that their deep red, dried blood spotted his white jacket.

He walked down the halls of the small hospital which were now scattered with makeshift beds of patients from the wreck. He felt exhausted as he entered his tiny but secluded office.

The nurse who had announced the accident earlier knocked and then entered. "Doc?"

"Yes, come in." He knew his voice betrayed his exhaustion.

"I overheard you say that your family left for the city this morning on the train. Have you heard anything from them yet?"

"No, and none of them were brought in today, so I can only hope it wasn't their train." He paused as he glanced at the picture of Beth and Luke. "Thanks for your concern."

"If there's anything I can do, please don't hesitate to ask," she said compassionately.

Most everyone who had worked with James found him extremely likeable. This feeling of concern was also an attribute of a small town and one of the reasons James liked it so well.

She disappeared behind the door.

James wasted no time tidying up details so he could be on his way home.

He walked slowly. He had used his energy on all the injured brought in today. So many of them had been his neighbors and children he had brought into the world. He felt spent, emotionally as well as physically. He hung his head as he walked and watched the dirt under his feet. He felt the chill air bite at his arms beneath the long-sleeve shirt. He had not worn the bloodstained white jacket home. Its appearance alone would frighten Beth, he had thought as he removed it and dropped it in the laundry cart.

As he neared home he sensed something. He raised his head and stopped in his tracks. There, in front of him, sat a state trooper car. The trooper, an old friend, sat on the porch swing bundled in a heavy, sheepskin-lined coat. James could not move his feet. They were frozen to the ground with fear, and it crept slowly up his spine.

The trooper rose and started down the steps.

James forced his feet to carry him toward the man, as he felt his body tense. "Evening, Doc."

"Cliff, what is it? What are you here to tell me?"

"Your family was aboard that train this morning, Doc. There had been a problem with the earlier train so it departed the station late." He paused.

James stared intently at the trooper.

"Your grandson was taken to Mercy, ninety miles away, with a concussion. I was told we only received the worst of the victims here in town." He paused again.

"Damn it, man. Go on," shouted James. Something inside told him he knew what was coming.

"Well, Doc . . . the rest of your family were killed. Your wife, son, and daughter-in-law. I'm sorry to have to bring you this news."

He stood motionless. His knees felt weak, but he willed himself to stay upright. "Thanks," he said and headed for the house.

Once inside, he sank into his favorite wingback chair with claws for feet. He sat still for almost fifteen minutes in a sort of void. He then decided to call Mercy Hospital.

When he reached for the telephone on the small table, he noticed Beth's note. "I'll love you forever."

The tears started at the corner of his eyes and began to roll down his face. He fell to his knees, and his body shock as the emotion of the loss poured from his very being.

"Why, why," he screamed to God. He sobbed, and shook for some time, until he felt he had drained himself of every drop of fluid in his body. His eyes felt swollen, and his nasal passage was clogged with mucus. He wiped the tip of his wet nose with the back of his hand, and then wiped his eyes with the corner of his shirt. He rose and dialed Mercy Hospital's number.

"Mercy Hospital. May I help you?" a young female voice answered.

"Michael Connectivich is a patient of yours. What's his condition? he asked somberly.

"I'll connect you to his nursing station, sir," the voice said. His call was transferred.

"Intensive care, Nurse Stranton speaking," an older, deeper female voice said.

"Michael Connectivich. What's his condition?"

"Are you a relative?" the voice asked.

"I'm his grandfather," James answered impatiently. He was not used to being questioned in his own world of medicine.

"He's here for observation, sir. The doctor's feel he'll be fine. His other grandparents are here with him," she said consolingly.

"Thank you," he said as he hung up the telephone.

He appeared at the hospital the next day. He entered the men's locker room to obtain a fresh white jacket. He paused at the mirror above the sink. He looked into the mirror and saw a face that showed great pain. The frown looking back at him spoke of sadness and his eyes were still red and swollen. He rinsed his face with cold water hoping to hasten the puffiness, but to no avail. He headed to the nurse's station to review the charts of his patients.

"Doc, what are you doing here? We all heard about your family. I'm so sorry for your loss." Nurse Garcia paused, and touched his shoulder. "You shouldn't have come to work, she scolded gently.

"What else is there for me now?" he asked quietly.

"Your grandson," she said. "I heard he was at Mercy."

He looked at her and turned to head down the hall to make his rounds. He knew if he answered he would begin to cry again. His heart was not in his profession today. He knew he would have to go to the morgue later today to make a positive identification of his family. He dreaded the thought of seeing his loved ones lying on a cold slab; lifeless.

There was nowhere he could turn that he was not constantly reminded of his loss, and he found no solace in the fact that hundreds of people in town had also lost family members.

The story of the wreck was on the front page of the newspaper he picked up. Ninety-seven People Reported Killed

Hundreds were injured when two trains collided.
Witnesses said forty cars were strewn about and
piled on top of each other in a mass of smoldering,
twisted steel. The fire raged as sulfur from the freight
train burned out of control for more than 48 hours.

He laid the paper down on the table in the small cafeteria. He could not read on, and the smell of the food around him began to nauseate him. One of his colleagues approached him as he was about to leave.

"Doc, sorry to hear about your family."

James didn't speak.

"Go home. We'll take care of your patients while you're away." Doctor O'Neal said sympathetically.

"I think I will," he said as tears began to well up in his eyes. He did his best to gain control over his emotions. "Thanks."

As he left, he removed his white jacket and set it on the counter of the nurses' station.

Months would pass, but the pain would not ease. He had filled out every form available and called every friend he knew in an effort to obtain custody of Michael, who was now out of the hospital and staying with his maternal grandparents in Boston.

He had returned to his work at the lab and the hospital, but life was not the same. His heart ached constantly.

Each night before bed he would look at Beth's belongings about the room. Her silver-handled brush had not been touched since she last used it. The note she had written and left by the telephone was a constant reminder of the intense love they had shared. As he lay in bed, unable to sleep, staring at the ceiling, he vowed to himself he would do anything and everything to get custody of his grandson. Michael was the only remaining thread of his family. His anger at God for taking all that he had, increased daily as the man within the body grew into an empty shell.

Let judgment run down as waters,
and righteousness as a mighty stream.

Amos 5:24

CHAPTER TWENTY-SIX

Two hours had slipped by, and Dr. Hess began to awaken. His stomach had decided it was its turn and was making its desires known. His mind imagined a steak two inches thick with a large baked potato with melted butter and sour cream rolling down its sides as it steamed from the heat. A green salad with a glass of deep burgundy wine would finish the picture, he thought. His mouth began to water, and he walked to the window to peer down the street, looking for a sign that would suggest this delicious fantasy might become reality.

"Ah," he said, as he focused in on the sign that read café. "That should do the trick." He picked up the bath towel that was sitting on the marble-top dresser which was next to the window. He paused before turning towards the door and laughed to himself as he realized he had just been looking at the view Bell had mentioned. Some view, he thought.

The bath was supposed to be at the end of the hall, he thought as he entered the hallway. He saw the staircase at one end, so it had to be at the other. He walked towards the only door at the end of the hall, which stood slightly ajar. He peeked in. It was dark. He then pushed the door open an inch or two and could barely make out the outline of a white porcelain sink.

"This must be it." He pushed the door open all the way and searched the wall for the light. He then saw a small piece of metal gleaming from the middle of the ceiling and pulled it. The small light bulb above shed little light in this tiny, closet like, closed-up room. There were no windows in the room. The white porcelain tub sat against a wall and had been modernized by adding a tall shower spout. The faded shower curtain reached only halfway around the tub. He shut the door, undressed, and laid his clothes on the toilet seat as he glanced up to the tank above his head. He felt as if he had gone back in time. He almost expected to see a horse and buggy in front of the bed and breakfast going about their daily lives. The town had a well-preserved, old-time feeling to it.

He peered into the mirror and noticed his tired-looking eyes. "Jet lag," he said. Then he looked around, wondering to himself to whom he was talking. "Boy, this place has a funny effect on people." He turned the worn chrome handles, and the screech from the rusty pipes was deafening. The sound settled down as the water flowed, and the pipe shook as if ready to come apart. He found it difficult to wash in this limited receptacle, which had definitely been designed for people of a smaller stature. The warm water felt good pounding on his body with a refreshing rhythm. He finished with a cold water finale that made his skin shiver with goose bumps. He wrapped the diminutive bath towel around him as far as it would go. The left side of his olive-colored hip and thigh peeked through as he walked. He picked up his clothing and opened the door enough to make sure he would not be providing an added attraction for anyone, and scurried down the hall to his room.

On his way out he laid the soiled slacks on the front desk and assumed Bell would recognize them. He could see her in the back room, but felt no need to bother her as she appeared busy with some sort of paperwork. Outside, the fresh breeze felt refreshing on his face and the air smelled of earth. He could hear the sounds of a small river close by as it ran noisily over the rocks within its path.

He walked towards the café sign with his huge steak in mind. Just before he reached the café, his nostrils caught the delicious smell of charcoal-broiled meat.

"Fantastic," he said as he walked in, knowing he was about to delight in what the hospital cooks had probably never set eyes on, let alone prepared.

He felt satisfied with the food he had ingested and his stomach ached from fullness as he drove the rented car through the darkness. The directions had been easy to follow, he thought as he pulled up to a little white house with a swing on the porch and gingerbread about the eaves of the second story. The moon was bright and showed the house off well. The lace curtains blew softly as the breeze pushed itself inside the open windows. He approached the front door, opened the screen door, and knocked several times. The door was opened by a wrinkled, gray-haired gentleman.

"Hello, Dr. Hess. I've been expecting you."

"Hello, Dr. Connectivich," he said as he held his hand out to the old Doc, as Bell had referred to him. Doc just waved him in as an usher might do.

"Come in, young man," he said as he opened the door wider.

He was slightly bent over with age and wore a gray sweater over a multi-toned green shirt and gray slacks. The slacks had a shininess to them, usually produced from years of wear. They appeared to be work pants of some sort, such as a janitor might wear on a daily basis. Maybe Doc liked working in his yard, which appeared well kept even in the darkness, or perhaps he had a garden out back, thought Dr. Hess as he sat down upon the deep green sofa covered in a heavily threaded, woven type of fabric. Nothing that could possibly be found in stores of today, he noted to himself. The arms and back of the couch was adorned with lace doilies. The fabric beneath the lace told of many years of comfortable use. Dr. Hess noticed the smell of an old person, sort of musty. He could never quite name the scent, or even go as far as to call it an odor, but he associated it with the many other aged people he had had as patients.

Dr. Hess watched as the old gentleman turned off the black-and-white television set, which appeared to be the only company he had, which was true for so many old people, he thought. He continued to watch quietly as Doc shuffled to sit down in a bright floral-print armchair with its delicately carved wooden legs and its claws connecting to the hardwood floor, also well worn.

Dr. Hess noticed a frame which sat on the table next to the armchair. He studied the picture for a moment. It held an attractive small blond boy who was holding a paint brush and was covered with splotches of paint from head to toe and crying as if in pain. He smiled and then glanced to the left of him at the fireplace. The mantle was crowded with pictures of people who most likely were Doc's family. "Is that your family?" he asked as he pointed to the mantle.

"Yes, it was." His voice revealed sadness.

Dr. Hess felt as if he had just stepped into quicksand. He intentionally changed the subject. "I've looked forward to meeting with you, Dr. Connectivich. While I was in college, I read about your work in cryogenics. You were quite a pioneer in that field."

"Yes, I guess *we* were pioneers. I say *we* because as you're probably aware, no one ever does anything alone. They've come a long way since, a very long way. Amazing, isn't it?"

Although his body was that of a very old gentleman, his mind seemed active and up-to-date with life. It was as if the body and mind had taken two different routes many years ago, thought Dr. Hess.

"That it is," replied Dr. Hess. "It's amazing. You and your associates made medical history. It was extremely daring, considering the period of time in which it all took place. I understand you actually had three people in a state of suspended animation. Are they still frozen?"

"Yes. Perhaps you should explain more about this little boy you were telling me about on the telephone."

The old gentleman moved restlessly in his chair, and Dr. Hess noticed he spoke with little emotion.

"I told you what happened during surgery when we spoke last week. I believe there's something here that connects this boy and yourself, Doctor. Only you can tell me if there might be anything to my thoughts."

"What exactly do you have in mind, Dr. Hess."

Dr. Hess felt the shrewd eyes of the old fellow watching him. He knew he'd have to dig for the information he wanted. Cryogenics had for so many years been regarded as a highly improbable science, and Dr. Hess knew the old man had been confronted with skeptics time and time again. He had probably grown defensive about the subject.

"I would like to know whom you have frozen, and what the particular circumstances were at the time. It might sound ridiculous to you, but you may have half of a soul locked up inside someone frozen in your laboratory while the other half is inside a little boy who needs the whole soul to be a completely normal person." He paused a minute. "I've been told you are and always have been a man of your convictions. I would like to believe I am as well."

That seemed to hit a keynote in the old fellow. His voice raised a notch or two.

"I'll tell you, son, your convictions change once you're old, crippled up with age and ready to leave this wretched world of ours." He leaned forward in his chair. "I've watched everyone I ever loved die. Here I sit in this house waiting to die, and I only have one relative left, who is in Boston." He picked up the picture of the paint-splattered boy. He looked at it fondly. Then he looked at Dr. Hess with a penetrating stare for a moment. He sat back in his chair. "If you think I sound bitter, you're damned right," he said. Then he lowered his voice. "I've spent my life giving life to this town and anyone else who needed it. In return, I've lost everything. I haven't had anyone for years." He paused. "I lost my wife, son and daughter-in-law in a train accident many years ago."

He looked so much older now than he had before the conversation had begun, thought Dr. Hess. "I'm sorry," he said as he tried to empathize with Dr. Connectivich.

"So is everyone. The town paid me with poultry and promises. You can't send a grandson to medical school with that, now can you?" He glanced at the boy's picture sadly as he held it in his lap.

"No, I don't suppose you can." So that was where the bitterness came from, he thought.

Doc's voice began to rise again. "I spent my life believing in God and doing what was right, and what have I got for it." He paused a long while. "You know son, ideals don't do us any good. God is within us, he gives us free will, but we're the ones who decide what judgment we deserve, good or bad. Maybe, I've done this to myself."

Dr. Hess felt the self-pity pour from the old man. He found himself in a difficult situation. He had heard Dr. Connectivich was a mellow, kind, easygoing fellow with an extremely alert mind. He now found himself in a room with an angry, bitter old man, drowning himself in self-pity. He felt himself sink deeper into the quicksand. An old man's abyss of anger, grief, sorrow and hatred towards all that had occurred to rob him of his loved ones. He found himself searching for a way to pull himself and this old doctor out of this pitiful hole of sorrow and self-pity.

"I'm sure a good deal of that is true, Dr. Connectivich, but I myself feel bound to do what I can to give a little boy a complete life, if that's possible. I believe that one of those bodies you have in suspended animation just might be holding Danny back from being complete. I know it's a radical thought, and perhaps a long shot, but isn't that what we doctors do?" He was doing a poor job of dealing with the old man's anger, and he knew it, but was determined to forge forward with his own ideals.

The old gentleman tilted his head a slight bit. Now Dr. Hess knew he had gotten his interest.

"Holding back? In what way?" His old voice crackled and displayed a defensive tone.

"A soul must be whole for a body to be undiminished. I feel that Danny, the little boy, is physically complete but spiritually incomplete, which is affecting his physical well-being. If one of your frozen bodies is holding the key, I need to know. Can you give me some detailed information regarding the occupants you have in suspended animation?"

The old fellow paused a long time, then straightened his back and replied, "I know who you're looking for."

This struck Dr. Hess oddly. How could he know?

Dr. Connectivich's voice became strong and forthcoming. "There are three people, two females and one male. The male was thirty-one years of age, dying from carcinoma. It completely surrounded the vital organs of his heart. His wife insisted on suspended animation. She believed that one day the medical community would find a cure."

Dr. Hess listened intently so as not to miss a single detail.

"We froze the body the moment he stopped breathing. That's too soon, you know. That's what being a *pioneer* gets you, mistakes for learning." He paused a second, cleared his throat on continued. "His family are all deceased now. Most of them died in that horrific train accident. It wiped out one-third of the town." He paused again as if to think about his comments. "The town was really growing until then. The town people the accident didn't get, the big cities did. People moved away in an attempt to forget, I guess."

Dr. Hess tolerated what seemed like an old fellows ramblings, while he waited for more pertinent information. He understood how Dr. Connectivich knew so quickly who it was that might be connected to Danny. There were laws now that prevented anything from being done to a body until it was pronounced clinically dead. That evidently was not the case at the time this young man had died. Dr. Connectivich spoke with what sounded like a guilty conscience. Dr. Hess said nothing but waited for him to continue.

"He called my name out just before dying."

Now the link was crystal clear. The boy had said the doctor's name during the operation. Dr. Hess could feel the excitement generating within him.

"That's it. That's the link." He did his best to hide the excitement he felt. He knew the bitter, old doctor would not be able to share the adventure with the same enthusiasm, although he continued to speak with exhilaration. "If this young man was frozen too soon, before his total soul could be released... well, Danny could have been reborn with only half his rightful soul."

The old doctor laughed scornfully. "Thank God for young, optimistic doctors."

Dr. Hess was silent. He felt mocked. There was so much more to this old fellow than met the eye. Dr. Hess could see that the lonely world in which Dr. Connectivich existed in had become a living hell for him.

"What's the bottom line, Dr. Hess?" he said sarcastically.

"What are the chances of thawing this body? No one seems to care. They're all gone, you said so yourself. If we can give a little boy a normal life." He was excited, and it was beginning to sound like a sales pitch, he thought to himself. "There just may be half a chance, you know."

"Half a chance," the old man repeated. "What are the chances my grandson will go to medical school with what little I have to leave him?" He was being sarcastic again. The old doctor picked up the picture and stared at it intently. "I don't have long to live. Can you help my grandson get to medical school? You must have connections in the big city you practice in." His voice had changed, he was totally serious now. "After all, we all have our price, don't we doctor?"

Dr. Hess knew the old man was looking at him with that cold bitterness that ate at him daily.

"I'm sure I can arrange something. Does your grandson have the desire to become a doctor?"

"Just like his grampa." His voice was a mixture of sarcasm and pride. "He's all I've got. He's all I've had for the last twenty years." He paused. "Do I have your word on this? I won't be here to see it. I have less than six months left, I've been told."

"You have my word. I'll see he gets into medical school if he so desires."

They shook hands. It was not a difficult task for Dr. Hess. He had many connections at the colleges. He'd swing a scholarship or two for favors owed to him. Dr. Connectivich was certainly right about one thing, he thought: *we did indeed all have a price.*

The old doctor rose from his chair slowly and began towards the door with Dr. Hess behind. He opened the door and then the screen for Dr. Hess to pass in front of him.

"It's been a pleasure, son. I'll go more peacefully now. I hope your beliefs become fact. You think in big ways, my boy." His voice was more cheerful now.

"Well, it doesn't cost anything to dream, Doc. Thank you for seeing me. It's been my pleasure, Dr. Connectivich. You're considered nothing short of a genius, and now I understand why."

The old man laughed. "God be with you, young man. You'll need him."

Dr. Hess entered the car and drove slowly back to town. It was all rehearsed, he thought. It was too easy. He had felt the quicksand all the time he had been in the old man's presence. The intellect the man had once attained and used so wisely and lovingly was now aimed at only bitterness. Dr. Hess was grateful he had chosen his patients and hospital as his wife and family. No one could take that away from him as it had be taken from Dr. Connectivich, he thought.

He lay on the old, sunken mattress for a long time. He tossed and turned numerous times making the mattress springs squeak with song. The windows were open, which allowed the breeze to blow in gently. He continued to toss and turn, as did the lace panels on the windows. It was too easy, just too damned easy, he thought as he fought to go to sleep. Maybe it was meant to be, was his last thought before falling into a deep sleep.

Blessed are ye that hunger now: for ye shall be filled.
Blessed are ye that weep now: for ye shall laugh.

Luke 6:21

Chapter Twenty-Seven

Danny had been playing on the floor with his toy cars and trucks as Kelly visited with her mother, who had dropped by to see how her little angel was doing.

Danny had progressed extremely well since the operation. He was now ready to crawl with a steady balance. His speech had not improved much yet, but the doctors were very hopeful. Kelly and Jason had been prepared for the worst after surgery, hoping to avoid more disappointment. They received only positive expectation and encouragement from the doctors.

"He loves the new cars you bought him, Mom."

"I thought he could use more toys." She smiled in jest at Kelly.

"I'll be glad when all his curly hair grows back in, won't you?" said Kelly.

"Yes, but be patient. By the way, did your dad tell you he wants to retire. He says it's time to rest and take it easy after thirty-five years of working."

"What do you think about that, Mom? You don't sound very thrilled."

"Well, I really hate to see him sell the store. You know he started out selling old appliances he had repaired and built it up to the dealership. It's his baby. He's watched it grow and nursed it every inch of the way. I'm not sure he'll be able to occupy himself without the store to keep him busy." She laughed. "It's crazy. He says he wants to travel."

"Mom, that sounds great. That would be good for both of you. You've always wanted to travel. And, anyway, all mothers have to let go sometime. Maybe Dad is ready to let go."

"Kelly, dear, you know what a homebody he is. He never goes anywhere for the weekend, let alone travel."

"Mom, this is your chance. Grab it. Think of how much fun it would be to go to Hawaii or the Caribbean or even Europe. Heaven knows you both deserve it."

Just then Danny fell over onto his side and uttered a sharp cry. His muscles began contracting wildly.

Kelly dropped the iced tea she was holding and ran over to Danny.

"Mother, he's unconscious. Call Dr. Hess's office." Kelly grabbed the afghan off the sofa and covered Danny while her mother spoke with the nurse.

"Dear God, what now?" she cried as she watched Danny, afraid to move him.

He held his little arms tightly to his chest, stopped breathing, and began to turn purple.

"Mother," she yelled. "He's stopped breathing. What should I do?" Kelly began to panic. She had never encountered anything like this with Danny before.

"I'll call 911. Check his pulse and start mouth-to-mouth resuscitation. The ambulance will be here soon." She rushed to Kelly's side. She was just as frantic as Kelly, but knew she had to be strong for Kelly right now.

Before Kelly could begin, Danny began to breathe again, and the color slowly came back into his face. His muscles continued to contract, but not as violently as before and then relaxed.

"Thank God, he's breathing again," she said as she grabbed Danny up into her arms and held on tightly. She began rocking him back and forth. It seemed like such a long time before she heard the ambulance arrive and the paramedics come rushing in the door.

Kelly began to explain what had happened.

"It sounds like a seizure, but because of the different types, we won't administer any medication just yet," said the taller attendant.

They laid Danny on his back on the stretcher that had been brought in. The contractions had completely stopped now. They listened to his heart and took his pulse.

"It's over. He's gone to sleep, which is normal. We'll take him to the hospital. His heart is beating at the normal rate and all vitals are stable for now. Would you like to go with him in the ambulance?"

They covered Danny with a white blanket and fastened the restraining strap across his abdomen for safety.

"Yes. Mother, please follow and lock the house." Kelly walked out behind the attendants, forgetting everything else.

"Who's the doctor, ma'am? We'll radio in before arriving."

"Dr. Hess. He's out of town for a couple of days, I think. We've already called the doctor's office before you arrived." She spoke as if half-dazed.

They had secured the doors of the ambulance and sped off with the red light flashing but no siren.

Kelly's mother turned off the dinner that had been cooking on the stove and dialed Jason's office.

"Good afternoon, Howell, Ashley, and McMann. How may I direct your call?"

"May I speak to Mr. Ashley. This is his mother-in-law."

"I'm sorry, he is in a conference at the moment. May I take a message and have him return—"

"This is urgent, I need to speak to him now."

"Yes. Just a moment please."

Kelly's mother was put on hold. This must be a new secretary, she thought. She was aware that all secretaries had been alerted in the past to put through any of Jason's family members immediately.

"Yes, Mom. What is it?"

"Danny had a seizure. He's on his way to the hospital with Kelly."

"Okay. I'll meet you there." He hung up. No good-byes were given. There was no time to waste. In all the four years Danny had been their treasure, they had never experienced this with him.

When Jason entered the emergency room, Kelly was sitting by herself with her eyes reddened and puffy, her nose pink, and a pile of used tissues in her lap.

"Sweetheart," he hugged her, "tell me what happened."

"He's sleeping. The resident doctor said they're trying to reach Dr. Hess at home." She wiped the tears from her cheeks. "It was awful, Jason. Our little boy on the floor, jerking uncontrollably, and turning purple. He was doing so well before this." She began to sob heavily.

"Kelly, come on. Settle down, sweetheart. It'll be all right. Can I go see Danny?"

"No, they're moving him into intensive care to monitor the brain waves. They said they'd come and get us as soon as they were done."

Kelly's mother appeared at the entrance and came towards them. "How's Danny?"

Kelly blew her nose and tried to settle down as Jason explained the circumstances to Kelly's mother. They sat for nearly thirty minutes with nothing to say. They intently watched the clock on the wall as the minutes ticked slowly away.

"You may see Danny now," the nurse called to them from the edge of the hallway.

Jason stood next to Kelly in the elevator, staring at its stainless-steel walls as if drugged. His mind focused on the day they had spent at the park as he played with Danny on the grass. That was the day he had made his decision about the operation. Well, I guess we had to take the gamble, he thought.

The door opened, they stepped out and walked towards the door labeled ICU. The intensive care unit in Dallas had become a familiar setting, so here at home it wasn't foreign to them.

As they entered the room they saw their little angel hooked up to every monitor available to medical technology, or so it seemed. He was sleeping soundly. He didn't appear to be in pain. It appeared that Kelly felt better as she stood next to his bed with her hand upon his tiny chest, making sure he was breathing, even though the monitors clearly displayed that he was.

Dr. Hess nodded to Jason and Kelly as he entered the room. "Let's see what we have here."

Kelly turned, "Thank God, you're here. I thought you were out of town for a while."

He checked the chart on the table next to Danny's head, then the monitor readout and then Danny's breathing and pulse.

"I got back this morning. I'm glad I did, too."

That wasn't very reassuring as far as Kelly was concerned. It made it sound as if Danny was in great danger.

"He's sleeping peacefully now. I think what Danny experienced was a grand mal seizure. It is frightening to watch," he looked at

Kelly and smiled as he put his hand on top of hers with a pat and then removed it, "but it is basically harmless to the patient."

"Should we expect more of these?" Kelly asked with fear in her voice.

"We'll do some CAT-scans tomorrow. The small portion of tumor left in the brain may be causing complications."

"What type of complications?" Jason said.

"An abscess. Rapid growth causing pressure. I won't know for sure until I see the X-rays. I want you to go home and take care of Kelly, Jason. She seems very shaken."

"Okay." Jason put his arm around Kelly and headed out into the large room where his mother-in-law was waiting.

"He's okay for now, Mom. Dr. Hess will be with him for a while. Let's go home. They've got a lot of tests to do," Jason said as he led both women out of the waiting room.

Cast thy bread upon the water:
for thou shalt find it after many days.

Ecclesiastes 11:1

CHAPTER TWENTY-EIGHT

Kelly stood at the kitchen sink doing dishes. She had to wait for Jason to get home before going to the hospital. She hoped doing the dishes would act on her nerves in a restorative way. She felt constantly on edge. She tried her best to remain under control, but she could feel the frustration and anxiety mounting with each passing hour.

Why? Why did this have to be happening? Why to them? The strength she had worked so hard to build was no longer there. It had failed her this time. The anger rose as if the steam from a tea kettle was about to go off and there was no stopping it. Not even the tears that rolled down her face eased the pain within. It was too much. It was trying to explode.

She stood in front of the sink as she reached for the tall green water glass and looked at it like a pitcher eyeing the baseball and then, without a moment's hesitation, she flung it at the wall. It shattered into a hundred pieces. As the loud crash reached her ears, the tears poured out. The dam of welled-up tears gushed forward.

"Damn it, why? Why, God, must little Danny go through all this endlessly?" she yelled to the empty room surrounding her. "Have you no mercy?"

She sat at the table, laid her head down and sobbed heavily.

It was out, and she felt better, she thought. Then she realized she would have to vacuum very carefully to get up all the tiny pieces of glass. She knew she would hate every minute of the cleanup, telling herself over and over what a dumb trick it had been to begin with.

Jason had had a court appearance that morning, which could not have been postponed. They arrived at the hospital just after lunch, and the insulated carts that held the food trays lined the halls. Dr. Hess was to meet them in the conference room. As they opened the door he stood viewing the X-rays. He turned to greet them.

"Good afternoon," he said cheerfully.

Jason hoped that meant good news.

"Feeling better today, Kelly?"

"A little," she lied. "Thank you, Dr. Hess," she replied.

"We have administered several tests on Danny this morning," he said as he walked to stand in front of the first of two X-rays upon the large lite-up screen. He pointed to a dark round spot. Immediately Jason and Kelly knew what it was.

Dr. Hess pointed with his pen to a large opaque white spot on the film. "The tumor has grown back at an unbelievable rate, and is causing a great deal of pressure on Danny's brain. We have no choice this time. I've scheduled surgery for four o'clock this afternoon."

Kelly and Jason sat silent. It was as if a blanket of doom had covered them both. They had no desire to ask any questions that would only bring an answer they didn't care to hear. Dr. Hess broke the silence.

"The odds are extremely risky. We'll have to try for the whole damned thing this time."

There it was. They'd heard it, even without asking.

"Okay," Jason said. He took Kelly's hand and headed for the door. "We're going to see him. Okay, Doc?"

"Sure, but he's heavily sedated to prevent more seizures."

He might as well have signed the death certificate in their eyes. They knew going down that deep into the brain was extremely dangerous. It was only a one-in-a-million chance Danny could come out of it alive, let alone be normal.

Danny had been wheeled into the operating room a few moments before. Jason and Kelly settled into the plush waiting room.

"Jason, I'm approximately twelve weeks pregnant." Kelly's voice was dull and lifeless.

Jason looked at her. He didn't know how to react. Did she expect him to be happy or sad? He could see she needed a special reaction to this news, but he wasn't sure what was expected of him. Why the hell did she pick this particular time to tell me? He thought back to five years ago; the first time she had given him the same news. He had been exuberant for days. He walked over to the window, stared for several moments as Kelly sat on a thickly padded plaid chair and began to glance through a magazine.

He turned, walked to Kelly, knelt down, and kissed her forehead. "We'll call him Jacob." The subject was dropped at that point. Jason walked back to the window and stared out once again.

And fear not them which kill the body,
but are not able to kill the soul:
rather fear him which is able to destroy
both soul and body in hell.

Matthew 10:28

CHAPTER TWENTY-NINE

James sat at his round oak kitchen table and watched the birds in the grass as they searched for their afternoon's lunch. He sipped his tea slowly with all the time in the world at his feet. His mind returned to the young, dark-haired doctor who had caused quite a stir in his quiet, solitary habitat three days ago.

His mind flashed back to his younger days. He remembered he too had a love for life, meaning, family, beliefs, and a sense of urgency about everything in life. He too had hurried through life, anxious to live every second to its fullest. He too had given his all to humanity from the fire that burned inside with the help of his God-given talents. He had seen that in Dr. Hess.

His mind drifted to the day of the train accident, the tears, and the funerals. Tears welled up in his eyes as his mind searched through what was now history.

He could picture his small son running to him as he walked towards the house after a long day at the hospital and laboratory. He wiped the tears away with the back of his hand and took another drink of his now lukewarm tea.

He knew that the loss of his family was the point in time when his life no longer had any meaning. It wasn't the same to come home to an empty house in the following years.

He smiled as he recalled the visits he made to his only grandchild in Boston. He recalled with animosity that the Boston authorities had granted the maternal grandparents the right to raise the boy, feeling a busy doctor left all alone was not capable of the demanding task of bring up a small child.

He was clearly aware that his bitterness and disgust had begun with those events and grew day by day like a weed until it completely took over and strangled anything beautiful in a garden. He knew it had annihilated anything that remained in him that had been charismatic or positive, until at last, only anger, sorrow and resentment were left.

When he had become sickly and too old to practice medicine, he no longer had any meaning to his life. He laughed to himself as he remembered the day his closest colleague, Henry, had informed him he only had a year, at the most, to live. It felt like a release of a prison sentence, rather than a death sentence. He recalled the feeling of relief while sitting in Henry's big-city doctor's office. He suddenly could again appreciate the beautiful wood paneling on the walls with enormous matching bookcases overflowing with medical books, half probably never opened. Henry had done well in his profession. Now, James had something to look forward too. The end of his suffering was in sight.

He had hope that Michael would be as successful once he finished medical school. He once again felt relief wash over him. At least, I was able to arrange for him to go to school, he thought.

He rose from the table and set his teacup on the sink. As he left the house, he left the door unlocked without giving it a second thought. He knew he was old and sickly but refused to give up his habit of walking to town each day. It served two purposes as far as he was concerned. It used most of the days' time up, and it made him very tired at the end of the day. He would fall asleep easily, and that pleased him.

Most of the people he knew well were as old as he. The offspring, most of whom he had delivered, were respectful of the elderly fellow, even though he knew he had outlived his purpose.

Once into town, he headed towards the lab. It was a brick building of sturdy construction and showed little wear from the years it had stood and served its town. He held tightly to the pipe railing to boost himself up the three concrete steps. He opened the metal door and viewed the stagnant, unoccupied offices, the files and the books that lined the shelves at the far wall, turning yellow with age and nonuse. The dust lay thick on the furniture, almost like it was a protective covering. He headed towards the stairs in the back right corner that led to the cryogenic department of the lab. There had been no work done in this laboratory in many years. The larger city hospitals handled those efforts now. It only housed the three cryogenic capsules which held the bodies of the three people who had desperately wanted to believe in suspended animation and immortality.

Paul, the day watchman, sat inside his glassed-in office, watching over the monitors for the electric panels, and reading the daily newspaper with his feet upon the desk.

"Good afternoon, Paul."

"Well, Doc, how are you today?" he said as he removed his feet from the desk.

"Fine, fine," James said. "I hear Walt had problems with one of the panels last night," he lied.

"Gee, Doc, I hadn't heard anything about it."

"I think I'll take a look," he said as he walked across the room to the opposite wall, and started fiddling with the large metal covering to the electrical units which maintained the capsules constantly.

"Well, I don't know Doc. I mean, I know you know more about it than most since you set the thing up, but I'm sure Walt will have called an electrician out from the city or something." He fumbled with the words and moved out of Doc's way at the same time.

"No, it's just minor," the doctor insisted. "I told him I'd take a look."

"Well, okay, Doc. He'll be on duty before long. He comes in at five." He glanced at this watch. "It's almost three now, Doc. You sure you don't' want to wait for Walt? He might be of some help if you want to wait."

"No. No, I'll just look around for now. Thanks, Paul."

"Boy, old folks sure get set in their ways," Paul mumbled as he left the inner office. "I'll go check on the wiring at the capsule. Which one is it, Doc?"

"It's number three, Paul."

The doctor had the large metal covering completely off of panel three, as Paul reluctantly headed for the affected capsule.

Towards the back of the panel was another smaller metal box, its cover marked with the words, High Voltage. James walked over to the inner office and rustled through the top drawer of the desk. He found a flat-head screwdriver, shut the drawer, walked back to the huge electrical maze inside the panel and began prying at the metal box. The top flipped off with a loud bang.

Paul turned quickly and yelled at the doctor, "are you sure you don't want to wait for Walt, Doc?"

"I know what I'm doing," the old doctor yelled at Paul.

Paul then returned to checking the wiring at the base of capsule three.

Doc grabbed for the wires inside the smaller metal box and said, "forgive us for we know not what we do." He yanked the wires out with all the strength he had. Sparks flew and his body straightened out as 200 milliamps ran through it and the force threw his body against the opposite wall with great force.

Paul looked up toward the office, surprised by the noise. "Holy Shit!" He couldn't believe his eyes as he watched the old doctor flung against the wall, vibrating with electricity still running through every cell of his body, and *slipping slowly to the floor. Paul couldn't move. He stood petrified where he stood for what seemed like an eternity. His mouth hung open in amazement. Then, finally, he got hold of himself and ran to the door of the office. He stopped as his nostrils retracted. It stank of burned flesh. The doctor lay there in a half-sitting, half-sprawled position, arms and legs spread and his eyes staring into space as they remained open. The wiring smoked and sparked from inside the panel. Paul stared in disbelief. He reached for the phone, stretching over the desk, careful not to touch anything. He dialed the operator.*

"Operator," the voice stated.

"Betty?"

"Yes, it that you, Paul? You sound as if you've just seen a ghost." It was a joke around town, since he watched over the dead.

"Betty, send the police to the lab. There's been an accident." The fright in his voice was apparent.

"Sure Paul, right away." She paused. "Paul, what's going on over there?"

"Just send the police over here." He hung up the phone and backed out of the office and went to sit on the edge of one of the capsules to wait for the police to arrive. He felt nauseated at the smell of the burned flesh which permeated every inch of the room.

It was only a short time before the police were hurrying down the steps to the basement. Paul was still sitting on the capsule, staring at the limp body near the inner office.

"Shit Paul, what happened here?" said the sergeant as he shook Paul's shoulder.

"He said he knew what he was doing. He wanted to fix an electrical problem for capsule three." Paul continued to stare at Doc's body as he talked. He had gone into shock.

"Well, he fixed things all right. Poor Doc," said the sergeant as he surveyed the scene. He turned to one of the other policemen. "Take Paul home. We'll get the report later."

"Okay," the policemen shook his head at the sight and then took Paul by the arm and tugged. "Come on, Paul. It's done. There's nothing you can do here."

Paul rose slowly and reluctantly went with the policeman.

"Oh Paul," the sergeant shouted after him, "what about the capsules?"

"It's three, and it's gone," he mumbled in a low voice. Paul knew it would take days to replace the wiring, and the network of wiring was too old to

have had any emergency back-up system. The occupant was probably already half-thawed.

"He said it's gone," shouted the policeman as he led Paul up the stairs.

"Call Walt and get him down here," the sergeant said to the remaining officer, as he turned to survey the situation once more.

"Well, Doc, let's get this mess cleaned up," he said to the body as he knelt next to it and gently closed the eyes.

For I reckon that the sufferings of this present time
are not worthy to be compared with the glory
which shall be revealed in us.

Romans 8:18

CHAPTER THIRTY

Dr. Hess had entered the large double doors of the operating room, hands held up, facing him, dripping, waiting for a sterile towel to be tossed onto his hands for drying.

"Nurse, gloves." He held his hands out for her assistance. She put the second, far thicker pair of gloves over the first.

He walked to the head of the table and viewed the opening his resident had prepared.

"Scalpel."

The nurse laid it securely in the palm of his hand. He glanced up at the clock, five-ten. Then he returned to the grayish mass before him.

It's time and a half," he told the staff that stood around ready to assist. "Let's do some miracles, shall we?"

The staff smiled beneath the paper face masks at the doctor's sense of humor.

He proceeded to cut through the dura, trying to follow the same path as before. He handed the knife to the scrub nurse and requested the penfield one, and bipolar coagulator as he went deeper.

It was going well. No major blood vessels had gotten in the way, and the first path was easier to find than he had expected.

"Erika, can you bring in T-Rex please." He was referring to the huge Zeiss microscope which stood near seven feet tall, and which had to be wheeled from its corner in the operating room, toward the table.

The scrub nurse and Erika hurried to cover the monstrous object with a huge sterile, protective plastic bag while Dr. Hess checked the cardioscope, and listened to Danny's breathing.

"How's he doing?" he asked the anesthesiologist.

"Everything's fine."

151

When the microscope was in place, Dr. Hess moved forward to remove the protective plastic over each eye piece and let them drop to the floor. He adjusted the lens with the handles on each side until his view was perfect.

"Micro-knife and spatula."

The scrub nurse put them in his hands, being careful not to bump the scope.

Dr. Hess began dissecting through the delicate tissue. Meanwhile, the nurse handed the resident a syringe filled with saline for irrigation, and set a thin, round plastic tray which held saline soaked cotton patties of various sizes near the scope to provide easy access for the doctors.

He reached the tumor. "Spoon."

The nurse took the spatula from his left hand and replaced it with the micro spoon.

After several minutes Dr. Hess turned to the nurse with beads of sweat visible on his skin. "Can you wipe my forehead, please."

She dabbed with the blue disposable surgical towel being careful to not touch his forehead, which was not sterile, with her gloved hand then tossed the towel on the floor away from the sterile field.

The staff began to feel the tension as Dr. Hess dug in an effort to reach every bit of the tumor. They watched on the gigantic screens located high on the walls opposite the doctors, as Dr. Hess proceeded to extract the tumor. He dumped gray matter from the spoon onto the gauze sponge sitting near the opening. The mayo stand tray stood near the top of the head, and shaded the deeper regions.

"Move the tray back," he said calmly.

The nurse did so immediately. He proceeded to burrow in an effort to reach any tumor that remained.

"Knife." Again he cut deeper. As he cut, the blood shot out and covered the front of his blue gown.

"Coagulate that damn thing," he yelled at the resident.

The tension grew, and the silence was deafening.

The resident pushed his way through the instruments within the brain cavity. He held the tip of the coagulator ready to cap off the bleeding vessels.

Suddenly the breathing stopped and the bleeping of the cardioscope turned to a steady tone. The anesthesiologist hurried to adjust the flow of oxygen, but it didn't change Danny's condition.

"Dr. Hess, we have a problem. He's not breathing." He said calmly, but urgently.

Dr. Hess stood back. "Shit," he said under his breath. "Let's close him up, so he can be turned over. Erika call a code blue, and get T-Rex out of here."

He removed all the bloody cotton patties from inside the brain cavity then put the instruments he had been working with on the mayo tray. He held his hand out for the needle driver loaded with appropriate suture. The nurse handed the resident one as well. Both Dr. Hess and the resident stitched as quickly as they could. First the dura was closed, then the skull cap was laid down, and finally the skin layer was closed with large, hurried stitches.

Dr. Hess looked at the clock. "Under four minutes to close, not bad. Let's get him out of the Mayfield and turn him over."

The resident took off his gloves, cradled Danny's head with one of his hands while he loosed the screws which held the head in place within the Mayfield apparatus. He did so quickly. Dr. Hess removed his gloves.

"Ready to turn?" he asked the resident.

"Ready."

Erika looked at the clock in order to document the actions being taken for the record.

"Five fifty-eight," she said so that everyone was aware of the timing of events. She typed the information into the record on the computer.

Dr. Hess knew all who were present, including himself were silently praying this boy would again begin to breathe before CPR was started and the little boy's ribs would be broken under the pressure of compressions. The nurse at his side was ready to begin CPR once told to do so. Dr. Hess was aware that she had a son about the age of Danny at home, and guessed she would relate this small, helpless boy to her own child.

"Okay, let's start CPR," he said loudly as he backed away from the lifeless body.

The anesthesiologist monitored Danny's vital signs, while the sound of cracking ribs were heard as compressions continued. A second nurse replaced the first since doing compressions on anyone was an exhausting procedure.

"Let's try the defibrillator," he said loudly.

The code blue team had brought in the code cart and was ready with the AED machine. Dr. Hess put the pads on Danny's chest and left side. The team followed the instructions spoken by the AED machine, and once everyone was clear of the body, it sent an electrical charge through Danny's body. The small body jumped into the air and landed. Nothing. The machine analyzed the body once again, and sent another charge through Danny's body.

"Six-O-Two." Erika announced the time once more, while simultaneously making notes in her nurses log. She left her chair at the computer and went to the group of people gathered around the body. "Doctor, four minutes have passed. I think he's gone," she said.

He ignored her completely. "One more time," he said in a frantic voice. Again, the body jumped and nothing. He stood and stared at the body for a long moment.

"Okay, I guess that's it," he said. All hope gone from his voice. "How long Erika?"

"Six minutes, sir," she replied.

Dr. Hess looked at the resident who was watching him intently. "I think we're done here." His voice carried the tone of defeat. He turned to leave the room. What could have gone wrong, he thought. Danny had such a strong heart.

"Wait," said anesthesiologist. The cardioscope sounded a tiny bleep, and the line on the monitor showed a speck of movement.

"Doctor," one of the nurses yelled softly. He turned to watch as the cardioscope began to bleep and the line bounced with life.

"Doctor, he's coming back," said Bill, half-shocked, half-fearful.

It had been much too long. There would have to be brain damage. It was inevitable.

The bleep grew louder and stronger, and the breathing bag began its rhythmical movements once more.

Dr. Hess came back beside the table and lifted Danny's eyelids looking at the pupils.

"Gloves please."

Erika opened two packages of gloves in sterile fashion and tossed them on the mayo stand which was the only surface in the room that had not yet been cleared of instruments, or touched by anyone.

"Can you get a large helmet up here stat, Erika? And, give me some anti-bacterial ointment and several gauze rolls."

She didn't answer but moved quickly to fulfill his requests.

He looked at the resident who was putting on his gloves. "We're going to wrap the head, put the gauze on for padding and the helmet for protection. We'll watch him for the next 24 hours, and if all goes well, we'll bring him back in and tack the cranial flap down, wrap the ribs and hope for the best."

The resident nodded, but uttered no words. The feeling of hopelessness filled the room. It was common knowledge in the medical community that there was usually extreme brain damage caused by the lack of oxygen during the time Danny had stopped breathing.

Once Danny's head was protected by the application of the helmet Dr. Hess left the room. He saw Dr. Hedding standing at the sink outside the room, scrubbing for his next case.

"How'd it go, Stan?"

"Not good," he said quietly. "He was gone for over six minutes, at least. It'll take a hell of a lot of prayer, a miracle, or pure talent, to pull this one out, Vic." He didn't grin, even though it sounded like a joke.

"Hell, that's too bad, Stan. Don't take it too hard Stan, it happens."

"Yeah," he said as he sighed. He walked away.

He continued on his way to the locker room. As he sank into the armchair nearest the telephone, his buttocks rested at the edge of the chair, his legs sprawled out in front of him, he laid back in the chair, raised his hands to his forehead and ran them back against the top of his skull with a long, heavy sigh of defeat. After a few moments he picked up the telephone, dialed, and began to dictate the procedure of the operation to the tape recorder at the other end located in medical records. Once finished he hung up the phone, and reviewed the case in his mind, wondering what had happened.

It was near eight when Dr. Hess walked into the waiting room. He had removed the blood-covered surgical clothing and had changed into his street clothes and white clinic jacket.

Kelly and Jason sat and stared at the television but had no idea what was on. They turned and rose the moment they heard the door open and realized it was Dr. Hess.

Dr. Hess looked around to be sure no one was close enough to hear what he was about to say, except Jason and Kelly. No one was. He approached them. "Sit, please."

He began. "I'm pretty sure we got it all this time," he told them. "However, we had some complications." He paused. "Danny suffered a cardiac arrest during the operation."

Kelly gasped and put her hand over her mouth.

"I have to be honest with you. It lasted approximately six minutes, so it's a matter of time before we know how Danny will fare. The tumor is gone, but we don't know if or how extensive the damage might be to the brain because of the lack of oxygen. He's still under the anesthetic and will be for a while. He won't be awake for several hours and even after he wakes from the anesthesia we need to keep him sedated." He hesitated before continuing to tell what was to occur next. "We had to put the cranial flap on without securing it, so we'll have to take him back to the operating room in approximately forty-eight hours to secure the flap. Meanwhile he has a helmet on to protect his head."

Kelly wiped the tears from her eyes.

Jason put his arm around her, hoping it would give her strength.

"Does that mean that he might end up a vegetable?" she asked in a shaky voice.

"We won't be able to give you any information one way or the other until Danny's woken up and we can evaluate him. I'm sorry I can't give more than that right now."

"What are his chances, Doc?" said Jason.

"Chances of what?"

"Of survival, I guess."

"Again, I can't tell you anything, we just have to watch him for the next twenty-four to forty-eight hours. I'm sorry I can't tell you more."

Silence filled the air for several minutes.

"Perhaps it would be best for both of you to get a good night's sleep and return in the morning. Danny's in recovery right now, and will go up to the intensive care unit, but we'll keep him sedated so he won't be awake enough to know you're there. Get some rest. You've both been through a lot."

"Okay. Thank you Dr. Hess," said Jason as he and Kelly followed Dr. Hess out of the waiting room and headed home for the night.

Be not faithless, but believing.

John 20:27

CHAPTER THIRTY-ONE

Dr. Hess sat in his well-padded desk chair with his head back, resting it upon the high back. His eyes were closed, and his arms were stretched along the arms of the chair. He felt exhausted and reluctant to go home. It had been a long day, and he hated to leave Danny all alone. He had grown greatly attached to this little boy, probably too much so, he thought.

After several minutes had passed, he opened his eyes slowly, sat up, reached for the in-house telephone, and proceeded to arrange to use one of the night resident's beds.

As he put down the receiver, he had a feeling that more had happened than he had witnessed. He hurried to his locker to retrieve a notebook with Dr. Connectivich's number in it. He dialed, using the pay phone on the wall in the locker room.

The town operator answered.

"Dr. Connectivich, please," he said as the adrenaline began pumping through his body with anticipation.

"I'm sorry he cannot be reached at this time."

"It's urgent. I must speak to him."

"I'm sorry. I can connect you to the chief of police if you like."

"The chief of pol... why?" He then heard the phone ringing at the other end.

"Chief of Police here. Can I help you?" a husky voice said.

"Yes. This is Dr. Hess, and it's urgent that I speak to Dr. Connectivich right away."

"You're the city doctor who was here the other day, ain't you?"

"Yes, I'm the city doctor and you're the chief of police. Now, can I reach Dr. Connectivich, please? This is an urgent matter." He was growing extremely impatient.

"Sorry, that's not possible. He's dead. The Doc electrocuted himself tonight. It looks like he did it purposefully, too. He took capsule number-three with him."

Dr. Hess was shocked into silence.

"Are you there? asked the Officer. "You wouldn't know anything about this incident, would you?"

"Yes, I'm here, and no I wouldn't know anything about any incident." He paused.

"When did this incident happen?" he asked.

"Right around three o'clock. We've contacted his grandson already. Sorry to have to give out such news," the husky voice said now sounding regretful.

"Yeah, it's too bad. Thanks." Dr. Hess said before he hung up.

He leaned against the wall staring forward. Number three had been the young man. "Damn." He knew there was more to this situation. With the power cut off, he bet the body thawed quickly because the capsules were so antiquated. "Damn!"

Dr. Hess straightened up with renewed energy, his mind working wildly. The soul of the young man must have been released, then it went into Danny on the operating table. That was why Danny came back. Hell, why not? he thought. He could hardly contain his excitement at the idea. He knew he would count the minutes before he could test Danny's reactions when he woke up, but that would be a while yet.

"Jason," he said out loud. He'd tell Jason. He returned to his office and sat back in the overstuffed chair while his thoughts formulated. How would he recount this bizarre occurrence to Jason?

Let every soul be subject unto the higher powers.
For there is no power but of God: the powers that be
are ordained of God.

Romans 13:1

CHAPTER THIRTY-TWO

He dialed Jason's home.

"Jason, can you come down to the hospital? I need to talk to you. Don't tell Kelly where you're going." He paused. "I think Danny's going to be okay. I just want to discuss my beliefs with you again."

"Yeah sure. I'll be right there." Jason put down the phone, turned to Kelly, and said slowly, "that was Russ from the office. He needs to discuss a case of mine he's handling for me. I won't be long." He knew the excuse didn't hold much water, but hoped Kelly was too tired to pay much attention.

"Jason, must you go? It's rather late."

"Yeah, honey. He said it was very important, and it goes to trial tomorrow. I'll hurry back."

"Okay."

Jason could tell she wasn't thrilled with the idea. It was obvious from the look on her face. He knew she really didn't want to be alone at a time such as this, but he knew if Dr. Hess said it was important, it was.

Once Jason reached the hospital, he hurried down the halls. He didn't like the feeling that was overtaking him. His mind conjured visions of his little boy on the operating table, deep voices speaking and the staff staring with mouths open wide in amazement. He forced the visions from his mind. He wasn't sure he wanted to hear what he had a feeling he was about to hear.

He reached for the door knob of Dr. Hess's office, knocked, and paused to take a deep breath before entering.

"Hi, Dr. Hess, what's up?"

"Have a seat, Jason." He leaned forward on his desk. "Jason, something really strange has happened." He paused. "I know this will sound crazy to you, but hear me out before judging."

"Okay," said Jason. He could feel the sweat on the palm of his hands as he held onto the arms of the chair.

"Danny was gone for six minutes on that table today. After trying everything possible, I was ready to walk away. Then he came back. No one was near him, he just came back by himself." Dr. Hess paused, looking intently at Jason. When no response came from Jason, he continued.

"This evening I found out that at exactly the same time Danny was gone, Dr. Connectivich had been electrocuted by pulling the wires on capsule three and taking it with him."

"What the hell is capsule three?" Jason asked. He knew his voice clearly stated he didn't like what he was hearing. He thought he had dismissed this entire horror story from his mind and now he felt forced to focus on it again.

"Capsule three held the body of a young man who I believe was connected to Danny."

"Connected how?" Jason said with more interest.

"I think the young man could have been frozen too soon, and his soul never completely released, so when your son was born or reborn he didn't have a complete soul."

Jason watched this well-educated doctor of medicine speak like some crazy witch doctor.

Dr. Hess got up from his chair and began pacing back and forth behind his desk, his mind formulating what had happened. He stopped and looked down at Jason.

"Jason, don't you see? That's why Danny came back. The young man would have thawed rapidly because of the old capsule. This was a capsule that was designed in the very beginning of the adventure through the frontier of cryogenics."

"Dr. Hess, you're working too hard, too much stress. You had better sit down and listen to what you're saying."

"Hell, Jason, I know it sounds unreal. But there's so much we humans can't conceive of in the world around us. Miracles happen all the time. One happened today in that very operating room. Jason, don't close down your open mind on me now."

"Dr. Hess, you're talking about my little boy." He paused and stood. "My flesh and blood. You are telling a spook story." He looked around the room.

Dr. Hess instinctively knew what Jason was looking for, even if Jason didn't. "Need a drink, Jason?"

"Yeah. Have you got one?"

Jason looked shaken. Dr. Hess walked over to a cabinet and pulled out a tray holding a decanter and glasses.

"Bourbon okay?"

"Sure, just right." Jason drank the shot of liquid fire in one swallow. He felt it warm the insides as it went down. Jason never drank much, but he held the glass out toward Dr. Hess for a refill.

As Dr. Hess poured once again, he spoke, "Jason, why not? Why in the hell is it impossible?"

"It's not, and I guess that's what scares me," he replied, feeling like a shaken kid.

They went over it again. Jason was more willing to accept such a theory the second time. He knew the bourbon was helping to open his mind, but had no problem with that. He knew he couldn't share this information with Kelly. She had been through enough with the operation, now with her being twelve weeks pregnant, she didn't need any more shocks.

Dr. Hess suggested they go to ICU to check on Danny and put this discussion aside for now.

Jason and Dr. Hess entered the ICU unit. They saw Danny sleeping peacefully while the monitors about him made their quiet, reassuring noises.

"We'll have to wait until tomorrow, Jason. We can't tell anything about his condition until he wakes up."

"Okay. I'll be here first thing in the morning. Kelly will be here too. You'll have to be careful about what you say, she's twelve weeks pregnant, and can't take much more stress."

"I understand."

Jason touched Danny's cheek with his hand, leaned over the protective railing, kissed his tiny hand, and turned to go.

As one whom his mother comforteth,
so will I comfort you.

Isaiah 66:13

CHAPTER THIRTY-THREE

Kelly and Jason arrived early the next morning. Kelly stood next to Danny's bed while he slept and held his warm hand. Tears began to well up in her eyes.

Jason watched her, and recalled their conversation yesterday regarding what it would be like to lose their little boy. They had also discussed what life would be like if Danny woke up more mentally impaired than he already was. He knew Kelly had sacrificed so much in the past four years for her son. She had given up her career, and devoted her entire life to taking Danny to doctor's appointments, hospitals for testing, physical therapists, special education classes, and the list just went on and on. He could see the concern on her face, as she watched him sleep. They had no idea what to expect of Danny once he woke up, after all he had gone through the day before. He would be lying if he said it didn't scare him too, he thought.

"It'll be all right. You'll see," Jason said as he put his arm around Kelly's shoulder. His protective instinct was showing again. He wasn't even sure if it would, indeed, be all right this time.

Danny's eyes opened.

"Jason, look, Danny's awake."

"Yes, I see," he said with joy in his voice.

"How's my little boy?" Kelly gently asked.

He managed a slow smile, and closed his eyes.

"My boy, my sweet little boy," Jason said, as he ran the back of his fingers on Danny's soft cheek.

He opened his eyes again.

"Dad-dy," Danny said very quietly.

Jason turned to look at Kelly.

"I heard it, too. He said it clearly," she said with amazement on her face.

The nurse hurried over, and checked Danny's vital signs. "I think we should call Dr. Hess to let him know Danny is awake, don't you?"

"By all means," Jason said and turned his attention back to Danny. "How's my big boy doing?"

"Danny okay, Daddy," Danny said.

Jason couldn't believe his eyes or ears. Danny was speaking just like a normal four-and-a-half-year-old boy.

Dr. Hess had walked in and watched from the end of the bed. He then began checking all monitors and vital signs to be sure this was all real. He had a big grin on his face as he worked.

"Jason, Kelly, it's phenomenal. Danny spoke so clearly," he said.

Kelly had sat down. It appeared the physical strain was harder on her than anyone. Her pregnancy was progressing normally, but she grew tired so easily from all the stress she had endured.

"I think God has listened to and answered our prayers," said Kelly.

"I'm sure he has," replied Dr. Hess.

Life is for the doing today.

Edgar Cayce

CHAPTER THIRTY-FOUR

Danny improved rapidly within the next six months. He learned to talk perfectly, walk, run, and play just as a normal child his age did. They had adjusted to the miracle that had happened.

Tomorrow he would be five, and he was to have a huge birthday party. All the children he knew from the preschool he was now attending would be there.

Kelly and Jason were busy getting all the details worked out. Kelly's parents also helped and could hardly wait for tomorrow when Danny could finally enjoy his first real birthday party.

They had planned to have the party at the park Danny loved so much. It would be different now. Danny could run and play in the grass this time. He could easily name all of the animals up on the hill, and it would be difficult to tear him away from the amusement park nearby.

Danny had talked about his party all day. Kelly rocked him, and sang lullabies hoping it would help him go to sleep. She knew he was overflowing in anticipation of tomorrow, so she did her best to be patient with his restlessness.

The sun rose and Danny's eyes popped open as soon as the sun appeared in his room

"Daddy, Mommy," he yelled, as he ran into their room and bounced on the bed. "It's Saturday. It's my birthday. It's my party day. Hooray," he said, bouncing on their bed with excitement.

Jason grabbed Danny and tickled him. "No, I think we'll go fishing instead, little fellow. Who wants a party anyway?"

"No, Daddy. No. The animals are waiting for us. We have to go."

Jason laughed. "Okay, I guess we can't disappoint the animals." He laughed again, and tickled Danny some more. "I suppose we better have the party."

Danny hugged his father around the neck. "Goodie, goodie."

"Come on sweet man. I'll fix you some breakfast while Mommy sleeps a little longer."

"Thanks, Jason," Kelly said as she rolled cumbersomely to her other side.

Jason loved every minute Danny was awake. He was so full of life, thought Jason. It had indeed been a miracle. Even the media had asked for the story, but Jason and Kelly were not yet ready to share it with the rest of the world, even though it made the medical journals. Jason felt they had been through enough for now.

While the boys worked in the kitchen Kelly did her best to sleep, but the tiny fetus within her tossed and turned inside her making it impossible to get back to sleep.

She and Jason had discussed the upcoming birth. They were both very excited about having another child, but Kelly had expressed her concern and fear that carried over from the terrible moment the doctor had told her of the brain damage of their firstborn. He had tried to ease her fears, but still she struggled with the memory of Danny's birth.

She entered the kitchen in her bathrobe where the boys were busy fixing breakfast. Danny sat on the counter stirring the pancake mix with the help of his father.

"What's wrong, honey. Were we too noisy?" Jason asked.

"No, not really, there's just too much to do today. I thought I'd better get up and get going."

"Want some breakfast?" he asked as he lifted Danny off the counter onto the floor.

"No, thanks. I'm going to go get dressed." She turned to go back to her room.

But the fruit of the Spirit is love, joy, peace,
long suffering, gentleness, goodness, faith.

Galatians 5:22

CHAPTER THIRTY-FIVE

Kelly was delighted with the loud, happy children bouncing in the back of her car as she pulled into the park for Danny's first real birthday party. Her mother followed closely behind her with more jubilant youngsters. There were ten attending Danny's very first birthday party.

Kelly could see the multitude of different-colored balloons hanging from tree to tree, along with crepe paper waving in the soft breeze. It was a wonderfully warm day.

"Look, Danny, there's Daddy, and it looks like he's all ready for your party."

"Wow," Danny said. "Hurry, Mommy, hurry."

"Yes, sweetheart. Just let me park." She pulled into a parking spot, and the children couldn't get out fast enough.

"I see you survived the trip, Mom," Kelly said to her mother while she was getting out of the car.

"They're so excited they can hardly stand it. They were discussing who gets to ride the pony first."

Kelly put her hand through her mother's arm and headed to the party area.

"Isn't it wonderful, Mom? Sometimes I can't believe he's the same little boy." She waved to Jason. "Hi, honey."

"Who rides on the pony first?" she heard him shout over the rambunctious children.

"Well, let's draw numbers. Come on, settle down, children," she said loudly in order to be heard.

They chose numbers, which Kelly had prepared ahead of time. The man who owned the ponies had cautioned Kelly about this very thing.

"I love watching you handle the children," he whispered in her ear. "I'm so proud of you." He rubbed her belly which protruded with life of another small being, who would be coming along any time now. "I can picture you handling four, maybe five, of my children." He laughed.

"You're dreaming, fellow," she teased. Her beautiful strawberry-blond hair blew in the soft breeze and touched his face gently.

"I love you," he again whispered in her ear.

They walked over to the picnic table Jason had laid out so carefully.

"What a beautiful cake," Kelly's mother said to Jason.

"Yeah, it is, isn't it, Mom? One of my secretaries at work made it. It's cool how she put all the animals on it with the train, isn't it?"

"Isn't it a bit big, Jason?" she asked.

"Well, sure it is, Mom. We had to make up for all the other birthdays, somehow." He laughed. "We had to get a big one to fit the train on. Besides, just think, now you get to take some home."

"Great. Just what we need at home, more sweets." Jason knew she loved sweets, and her chunky but well-proportioned body gave the secret away.

"Let's go help Kelly with the games, and the kids," Jason said, as he led the way.

The children finally had had enough of the pony once each had ridden twice. They went on to play games and eat cake and ice cream. After the three hired clowns had performed on the lawn, the children were driven up the hill in the miniature train to see the animals.

Danny could now name every animal, and he ran from cage to cage. He was having the time of his life.

It began to get late, and it was time to end the party and call it a day. Kelly was exhausted, so Jason and her mother did most of the cleanup while Kelly helped usher the correct child to the correct parents as they arrived to pick up their young.

Kelly's mom left with enough cake to last a month.

Kelly, Jason, and Danny packed into the car. Danny sat in the back seat next to some of his favorite birthday presents.

"You know what, Mommy and Daddy?" Danny said as adult as he could. "Today was the best day of my whole life."

"I'm glad, Danny. Next year we'll have another party, okay, big fellow," Jason said.

"Okay, Daddy." He laid his head against a huge, gray stuffed elephant he had received, closed his eyes, and was soon asleep.

Danny didn't wake up for dinner. Kelly changed him into his pajamas with Jason's help, and they put him to bed.

"I guess he's spent all his stored-up energy," Kelly said as she covered him with a fleece blanket.

"Yeah, he sure did have a great time, didn't he?" Jason leaned over and kissed his little man good night.

"How do you feel, sweetheart. Are you tired? Is junior kicking a lot?" Jason patted Kelly's tummy.

"Yeah, I'm bushed. I think I'll go to bed, too."

"But it's only nine."

"I know, but I'm really tired. You don't mind, do you?" She lumbered off towards the bedroom without waiting for Jason's answer.

"Okay, I'll come to bed in a while. Night, sweetheart."

The Lord shall preserve thy going out and thy coming in
From this time forth, and even forevermore.

Psalms 121:8

Chapter Thirty-Six

Morning came and Kelly was glad it was Sunday because Jason would be home another day. She always looked forward to his days off. She lay in bed, watching Jason sleep. She would be glad when she could again cuddle up to him without her huge belly keeping them at a distance. She listened and noticed the quiet. She turned to look at the clock next to her bed. It read eight o'clock. Danny was usually up and quietly watching television by now. She listened again. He can't still be asleep, she thought. She got out of bed, threw her robe around her shoulders, slipped her feet into the fuzzy slippers, and hurried into Danny's room.

There he lay. She knelt down to kiss him to see if he was going to wake up soon. His forehead was cold. She looked stunned. "Jason," she yelled. "Jason, come here quick."

He jumped out of bed, shaken into alertness by Kelly's yell.

"Jason," she yelled "Something's wrong with Danny."

Jason ran to her side, looked down at Danny, and immediately knew.

"It's okay, sweetheart, it's okay." He hugged Kelly and held her tight as the tears rolled down her cheeks. "He's in heaven now. He's gone to rest."

Kelly understood Jason was trying to comfort her, but she lost control and broke down into sobs. The tears flowed in rivers down her face.

"Come on, Kelly. I want you to come sit down on our bed. I'll take care of this."

Kelly took one last look at Danny and willingly went where Jason led.

Jason dialed Dr. Hess's home phone number.

"Hello," Dr. Hess said.

"Dr. Hess, its Jason. Danny appears to have died in his sleep."

"I'll be right over. Don't call the police, Jason. I'll take care of it." He hung up without any good-byes.

Jason then went to Danny's bed and knelt down next to him. The tears streamed down his face silently, as Jason stroked Danny's thick, dark brown hair. "My little man, braver than anyone I've ever known." He wiped the wet tears from his cheeks with the back of his hand. With the forefingers of his other hand, he traced Danny's little hand that lay still on the pillow.

He heard Kelly calling from the bedroom. He reluctantly got up and went to her. He knew he would have to be the strong one in order to get Kelly through this. He knew this was the last thing she needed right now. What if she went into labor, he thought, as he went to her. He pushed it out of his mind. It was a negative thought.

"Jason," she said as he entered, "Danny's gone forever isn't he?"

"Yes, my darling. Danny is gone forever. He's with God now."

He held her tight as she shook while sobbing into his shoulder. He wondered if, indeed, there was a heaven and if Danny was really safe and sound with God? He felt it to be true.

There was a knock on the door.

"That must be Dr. Hess," he said. "You try to take it easy, sweetheart." He gently released her and left to answer the door.

Dr. Hess followed Jason to Danny's room. He checked for a pulse. Nothing.

"It does appear Danny died in his sleep. Where's the phone? You go stay with Kelly. She needs you. I'll take care of Danny."

"Thanks," Jason said as he pointed the way to the phone, and headed toward his room to be with Kelly.

Come unto me, all ye that labour and are heavy laden,
and I will give you rest.

Matthew 11:28

Chapter Thirty-Seven

The large, shiny, black door to the limousine slammed shut. Neither Kelly nor Jason could restrain their tears. Jason held Kelly close with his arm around her shoulder.

He turned and took one last look out the back window to silently say good-bye to the golden coffin that held his little man. He was grateful it was all handled so quickly.

He would resume work tomorrow, he thought. He was trying hard to fight the sorrow. He had loved his brown-haired boy so very much.

"Why, Jason? Why, do you think God took him after granting him a full life for such a short time?" Kelly said.

The limousine began to slowly pull away from the burial site. Jason turned forward again and stared at the space in front of him.

"God made Danny a whole person. We have that to be thankful for." He paused and wiped the tears from his eyes. "I guess it's just a one-way passage for any of us, sweetheart. Danny had his own path to follow and now he is moving forward on that path with God at his side." He paused.

He knew the answer wouldn't seem like much right now. No answer would. They rode in silence. There was nothing that would ease their pain. Only with time would they learn to accept and move on.

Kelly's mother and father were having a reception afterward at their house. Jason didn't feel Kelly was physically or emotionally strong enough to attend. She was already one week overdue with the baby, and her obstetrician had told Jason of his concern about the emotional stress Kelly was experiencing.

Once they retrieved their car, they went right home. Protocol would have to be overlooked this time, Jason thought.

Danny's room would be shut off until Kelly was stronger. Jason knew it would be a while before she had the emotional strength to go through it. Only the nursery spoke of hope and moving on with life. Both he and Kelly were drained at the present time.

Jason fixed himself a drink as soon as he had gotten home and slid off his jacket.

"Would you like a very light drink, Kelly? Maybe an Amaretto and seven?" he asked.

"Maybe a real light one. I guess it would be better than a sedative." The tears came often. Jason knew she was trying to be strong. Her nose was red and nearly raw from the rough tissues.

"Put your feet up, Kelly. It'll help you to relax," he said as he brought the drink over to her.

The sun began to set, and evening was taking over the sky.

Kelly grabbed for Jason's hand and held it next to her face. "Jason, I'd like to think mother is right about reincarnation," Kelly said, as she stared at the blank space of white wall just ahead of her. "At least then Danny will be born again, only this time as a complete, and whole being from his first breath."

"Maybe, It is a pleasant thought to hold onto sweetheart." He leaned over to kiss the tears from her cheeks.

Jason then released Kelly's hand and turned while wiping the tears from his own cheeks. He walked to the stereo system, turned on some soft music then returned to Kelly. They silently sat next to one another for a long time, somehow comforting each other to some small extent.

My God, my God, why hast thou forsaken me?
Why are thou so far from helping me, and
from the words of my roaring?

Psalms 22:1

CHAPTER THIRTY-EIGHT

Kelly felt like cursing the sun when it crept in through the heavy drapes every morning. She forced her eyes to stay shut against their will. When her eyes finally succeeded, she lay in her warm bed, staring toward the ceiling. Tears now automatically rolled down the side of her temples and fell quietly upon the pillow. She felt as if she had done nothing but cry for the last several years. If only life would take a different turn, she thought.

She was all alone. Jason had gone off to work already. She could let down the charade and cry openly for the absence of her precious little boy.

He was not there to come and bounce on their bed. He was not there to read to. He was not there.

The life inside her kicked. She ignored it. She was so very fearful of another handicapped child.

She cried and spoke softly. "Why, God? Why did he have to die?" The tears ran like rivers onto her pillow, until there were several huge wet spots. "Why, after all he'd been through?"

She turned over and sobbed into her wet pillow as her body shook with the heartfelt pain. She would cry herself dry, and then, and only then, could she force herself to go on about the chore of living.

She climbed out of the shower. Her bulging stomach still held droplets of water on top of it. She heard an inner pop. The water gushed down the sides of her legs and onto the soft blue carpeting below. She quickly took the towel she had been drying herself with, and held it between her legs until the amniotic fluid subsided somewhat.

She grabbed her robe from the back of the bathroom door. She put the robe on, and rushed to grab a dry towel. She held it between her legs to catch the dripping amniotic fluid, and walked to the telephone.

"Mother, it's time. My water has broken. Can you come over?"

"Oh, darling, of course. Have you called Jason?"

"No, he's in court this morning, I think."

"I'll call his office and let him or his secretary know. You call your doctor, and I'll be right over."

"Thanks, Mom, and please hurry. I don't want to be alone." She hung up. The fluid came in small gushes, especially when she moved.

She called her obstetrician, and then tried to get dressed. Her long red hair was still wet. She would have to blow dry it before she put it up, she thought.

She could feel the fear begin as the small pains commenced.

The doorbell rang. It was her mother. She hugged her mother and then her father who followed behind.

"Dad, can you take my suitcase to the car, please? It's in the hallway."

"Certainly, honey." He picked it up and headed for the door.

"Oh mother, I'm scared," she said as she sat down.

"Scared of what, sweetheart? You've been through all this before." She looked at Kelly quizzically.

"I'm so afraid this child will be handicapped, too. I haven't shared that with Jason. He'd get angry with me."

Her mother knelt down and took Kelly's hand in her own. "Sweetheart, God will watch over you, and whatever happens is his will. It's meant to be. We can only try to be as strong as we are able and have faith in God."

"Mother, do you really believe in reincarnation?" Kelly asked, as she held her belly as the pains grew stronger.

"Kelly, does it matter? Whether it is or not, God still controls all things. Nothing can or ever will replace your little Danny. Not this baby or any other." She lifted Kelly's head up with her hand under Kelly's chin. "It's time to be joyous, Kelly. God's given you another miracle. Now let's go and get on with it. That baby is coming whether you agree to it or not." She smiled a loving smile. "Jason is meeting us at the hospital." She helped Kelly up from the chair.

Kelly kissed her mother's cheek. "Parents are special, aren't they?"

"I think so Kelly," she said as she helped Kelly out the door and to the car.

Every end is a new beginning.

Marianne Williamson

CHAPTER THIRTY-NINE

Kelly was admitted and Jason helped her time the pains on the way up to the labor and delivery department. Her parents would stay outside in the waiting room.

"Well, Kelly, my dearest. Is it a boy or a girl you're going to give me this time?" Jason said cheerfully, trying to make Kelly smile.

"I hope a girl," she said soberly.

"Why a girl? he asked.

"Why not? she said and smiled as a new contraction began.

"Well, how is a girl going to like being called Jacob," he teased her. "That's the only name we've picked out, you know."

"No, that's the only name you've picked out." She paused and let the contraction she was experiencing pass. "Did you know that that name means to replace another?" she asked.

"No."

"Well, it does, and no one can ever replace Danny. This is all new. You need to choose another name."

He looked at her in amazement. Was this the same person who cried all day while he was gone and tried to hide it all night while he was home. He smiled. It was the red nose that always gave it away. The sound of Kelly's groan and her grimace brought him back to the moment. "How are the pains, sweetheart?"

"Getting stronger and faster all the time."

The nurse who pushed her wheelchair smiled at Jason. "Is it worth messing the sheets on the bed or should we take her right to delivery?" the nurse asked, but was teasing.

Jason answered as Kelly started forcing breathes out as the pain grew stronger. "With her past record, you'd better take her to delivery."

Kelly grimaced with pain as a contraction hit its climax and then began to ease. She grabbed for Jason's hand and squeezed it.

As soon as she was in the bed, Dr. Nagel checked her vaginally. She was eight centimeters dilated and progressing quickly. "Better get her to delivery. Okay, Kelly, don't push until we get you to the delivery room. That baby will be here soon," said the doctor.

Dr. Nagel left to prepare for the delivery, and left Kelly with the nurse and Jason to coach her.

Within the hour, Kelly delivered a baby girl, eight pounds, two ounces, with lots of red hair standing on end.

"You did a good job, sweetheart," Jason said as he knelt and kissed her forehead.

The doctor finished stitching the episiotomy, cleaned her up with a moist gauze sponge, and helped the nurse remove her legs from the stirrups. "The nurse will take you to your room, and I'll bring the baby in soon. I'll do the testing," he said while he removed the instruments and mayo stand from the end of the table.

Kelly looked at Jason. He could see the apprehension on her face. "Sweetheart, it's going to be okay," he said while brushing her long hair from the side of her face.

It felt like an eternity, before she heard the doctor approaching the room. Jason had been pacing at the end of the bed, which made Kelly feel more nervous about what the doctor would say about the newborn testing. She watched the door, hoping to see the answer in his face before he spoke.

Dr. Nagel carried the small bundle in a pink receiving blanket. He leaned over the railing of Kelly's bed and handed the tiny bundle to her. "She's perfect. All she needs now is a name." He smiled at the new parents.

Tears of happiness formed in Kelly's eyes. She opened the pink blanket wide and looked down on her new miracle. Then she looked up to Jason, "is Angela okay, and we'll call her Angel?"

"That's exactly what I was thinking," he said and beamed with pride at the little girl. "It's perfect, just perfect."

END

CPSIA information can be obtained
at www.ICGtesting.com
Printed in the USA
BVHW032012230619
551755BV00003B/202/P